2048 BCE
THE EYE OF HORUS

DEREK BEAUGARDE

Published in 2023 by Corkerhill Press

Paperback: 978-1-7393929-5-6
eBook: 978-1-7393929-9-4

A CIP catalogue copy of this book can be found in the British Library and the National Library of Scotland.

Published with the help of Indie Authors World

Exodus 7:5 (New Testament and Psalms
© The Gideon's International)

The Egyptians shall know that I am the Lord, when I
stretch out My hand on Egypt and bring out the sons
of Israel from their midst.

For my beloved grandsons Cailean and Lewis.

Acknowledgments

The author wishes to acknowledge the valued assistance of Indie Authors World in the publishing of this book. The author also wishes to thank his editor Gillian Murphy and his reviewer Anita Dow for their usual critical endeavours.

Also thanks to fellow alumni Sir Dirk Bogarde for the pseudonym and Allan Glen's School for the superb education. The author wishes to ascertain this is a work of fiction and any relation to any person living or dead is purely coincidental.

2048 BCE
THE EYE OF HORUS

Derek Beaugarde's compelling prequel to

2112
REVELATION

Derek Beaugarde's thrilling sequel to

2084
THE END OF DAYS

BOOK 1: GENESIS

BOOK 2: EXODUS

BOOK 4: THE EYE OF HORUS

Prologue

On 26 May 2084 planet Earth was utterly destroyed. The rogue comet Schenkler HMM2, inadvertently discovered back in 2081, travelling through the Kuiper Belt, slammed destructively into the Pacific Ocean near the Marianas Trench. Earth and its moon were vapourised, along with all life on the planet. Due to the concerted efforts of world governments, a small surviving colony was established at Capitol Base on Mars, in the foothills of the Western Arabia Terra.

In 2112, a geological survey, led by Jack Sinclair and his assistant Atlanta Caie into the unexplored Martian hinterland, discovered three intricately carved iron pyrites pyramids at the base of the Uranius Patera volcano, about 30 kilometres from Olympus Mons. They uncovered the Revelation of the Seal, which revealed there had been a highly sophisticated Martian hominid culture on the red planet dating back over three million years.

The transcriptions from the pyramid walls detailed Mars was a dying planet. The red planet's atmosphere had been fatally damaged by a giant meteorite strike. The Martians detailed this had occurred in the region of the deep Valles Marineris canyon, gouged out by the meteorite. Life-sustaining oxygen gradually leaked from the Martian atmosphere, like air from a balloon with a small pin-prick. All life forms on Mars were destined for extinction.

Around two million years ago, the Martians discovered Earth, their *blue traveller,* contained a viable, breathable, and oxygen-rich atmosphere and they started to visit the blue planet to conduct research. Their plan had been to overtake and then re-populate Earth with mass migration from Mars.

The problem they encountered was Earth's gravity. The

gravity on Mars was only thirty-eight percent that of Earth. The tall, slender skeletal Martian hominid discovered in the iron mine under the pyramids was deemed atypical at 2.5 metres tall. It was calculated it weighed about 80 kilograms on Mars, but a crushing 210 kilograms on Earth. The Martians could not survive on Earth and they were slowly becoming extinct on Mars.

The Martians embarked on a program of transporting samples of Earth's alien life forms back to Mars. A sort of two million-year-old *alien abduction*. Their plan was to mix their own genetic DNA with various species, *the last of the great beings of the red traveller sowed his seed among the beings of the blue traveller*. The Martians interbreeding program had multiple failures, however, among the primate species, they began to have a measure of success.

Various transmutations were transplanted back on Earth; Homo erectus, Homo Neanderthalensis, Homo Australopithecus, et cetera. It appears the Martians successfully interbred and nurtured one particular species, around 2 million years ago. *Many seeds failed. One seed thrived and then there was the new being.*

*

Homo sapiens. Modern humans were descended from the Martian hominids. *The Missing Link*. The Martians kept a close eye on the evolution of humans over many millennia, visiting Earth on many occasions to determine the continued success of their project.

However, life continued towards extinction on their once abundant red planet. Their last visits were made to Earth during the reign of the Egyptian Pharaoh Mentuhotep II in 2048 BCE. The last Martians on the red planet died shortly after this period. Their rock carvings, which would act as a sort of 'Rosetta Stone', were passed on to Mentuhotep II for safe-keeping. They left behind the transcriptions on their pyrites pyramids, hoping one day mankind would venture out into the solar system and discover the origin of their species.

The Martian race called themselves the Bor-ak.

The Bor-ak had developed into a superior advanced technological race, thus having mastered space travel within the solar system. They were a peace-loving people, having eradicated war and strife over many past millennia.

The Bor-ak were also fervently religious people. They worshipped the Sun for its life-giving properties, however, in general, they believed in an omnipotent creator god, named Vor. Their god Vor lived in the heavens of Vor-maga. Vor-maga was the Bor-ak name for Olympus Mons, a truly sacred place for the Martian people.

*

When the deadly meteorite struck the Valles Marineris, it was the region of Mars where the main cities lay, including the capital Khor-Ek-Kada. Huge swathes of the Bor-ak population were wiped out instantly by the nuclear-type blast caused by the extinction event impact. Oceans and seas were evaporated and the red planet began its slow, painful death.

Many later Martian pyrites carvings concentrated on the need to save the Bor-ak gene pool by transmutation with the less evolved Earth-bound hominids. Homo sapiens, the smaller genetic cousins of the Bor-ak, became their success story. The pyrites scripts remained unfinished around 2048 BCE, having chronicled the final spacecraft departing the red planet of Mars to explore the continued evolutionary development of mankind. The spaceship, containing the seeds of the Bor-ak, their Martian DNA, would slingshot around their Vor sun and be blasted out of the solar system into deep space. The Bor-ak hoped one day they would find a new, habitable Mars-like planet somewhere out in the vast Milky Way galaxy.

Chapter 1

"Okay, Navigator, permission for Vor-maga I to leave red traveller orbit and steer a course for blue traveller."

"Yes, Commander, executing orbit exit. Thrust level one."

The huge spaceship, named by the Bor-ak after their sacred mountain, Vor Maga, pulled smoothly away from its Mars orbit with the low thrust of its fusion drive and accelerated towards the inner solar system and planet Earth. A journey of around five Earth months lay ahead of them.

The crew of the Vor-maga I numbered only thirty souls, leaving behind the last vestiges of their people on Mars. Everyone would be dead within a few months. The remaining oxygen in the atmosphere had all but bled out into space and the stockpiles of food and water were quickly running out. The Bor-ak crew were the last remaining survivors of a technically extinct species.

The ship carried the Bor-ak's great hope for the future. The hold was packed with deep-frozen Bor-ak DNA stockpiles, which would be used to repopulate a new habitable Mars-like planet lying in the 'Goldilocks zone' of some new distant Vor, a sun-god-star, out there in the Milky Way. After, what would be their last visit to Earth to investigate the development of the sub-Bor-ak, Homo sapiens, the plan was to slingshot around Vor and propel the spaceship out of the solar system.

Once safely through the Kuiper Belt, the crew would go into deep-freeze cryogenic capsules, possibly for millennia. The on board AI robotic computers would scan approaching star systems for suitable planets with Mars-like qualities of gravity, atmosphere and habitation. Crew members would be periodically awakened to check the Goldilocks planet and, if unsuitable, it would be back into the freezer and onto the next star system. It was a long shot, but it was all the Bor-ak had left to cling on to.

The Commander studied the computer for the archived

records on Bor-ak research visits to Earth. The previous visit was about 4,000 Martian years ago, about 10,000 BCE on Earth, where they found the blue planet emerging from an ice age. Most of the experimental hominids they had seeded on Earth had long become extinct.

There were effectively only two species remaining. The brutish Neanderthals, but they were only just hanging on in small disparate groups as a species and had not survived the ice age well. The smaller, more agile, intelligent Homo sapiens, the sub-Bor-aks, had retreated back from Northern Hemispheric regions and by the end of the ice age they were beginning to again migrate northwards, thriving and multiplying. The sub-Bor-aks even showed signs of rudimentary developments in protected city states in the warmer Middle Eastern climes. The end of the research visit concluded the Neanderthals were doomed to extinction and the sub-Bor-aks would become the premier species on the blue planet.

The Vor-maga I Commander's research remit was to establish if this was still the case and how advanced the sub-Bor-ak's had developed in those 4,000 Martian years. The female Navigator interrupted his thoughts.

"The ship's now free of our planet's gravitational pull, Commander."

"Take the fusion drive up to full thrust, Navigator. Sadly, we will never see our beloved red traveller again."

For all the crew on the bridge of the Vor-maga I, tears flowed freely.

Chapter 2

It was the start of Shemu, the hot Egyptian season of summer. A huge crowd gathered in the blazing afternoon sun in the main square laid out in front of Pharaoh's palace in Thebes. Palace emissaries had spent all of yesterday circulating in the capital city of Upper Mizraim, announcing Pharaoh would make an important speech. They waited expectantly, staring up at the ornately hieroglyph-painted wooden doors of the palace, and a great murmur arose as the tall doors were swung open by the Pharaonic guards.

Pharaoh strode out at the head of a phalanx of advisors, high priests, priestesses, wives, concubines and his numerous children and grandchildren. He stood imperiously on the pillared balcony at the top of the steep marble stairs, and as the crowd roared its adulation, he spread his arms wide, pointing his golden was-sceptre skyward towards Ra, the sun god. He was wearing his white crown, the symbol of Upper Egypt, atop his black and gold striped nemes, the traditional headgear of the monarch.

A slave stood behind Pharaoh, carrying a long pole with a banner depicting Montu, the falcon-headed god of war. The crowds cheered loud and long. After a few minutes milking the adulation, he lowered his sceptre and indicated with downward palms for silence. The murmur of the crowd quickly faded to an expectant silence.

"My fellow Mizris, citizens of Thebes, this day is the thirteenth anniversary of my ascendancy to the golden throne of Upper Mizraim, following the death of my father Intef, making me the sixth ruler of the Eleventh Dynasty. As a boy I was your Prince Nephepetre, the Lord of your rudder is Ra, the giver of life."

He paused for effect, pointing to the sun, and the crowd chanted back.

"The Lord of your rudder is Ra!"

"This morning, I attended the temple and lit burning oils, frankincense and myrrh to honour my father Intef, the god-king , now in the heavens alongside our sacred ancestors. I prayed to Ra for a long life for myself, Mentuhotep, to serve my people most gloriously and for the life of my eldest son, Prince Mentuhotep, who will eventually succeed me as Pharaoh. Glory to Ra on this first day of Shemu."

The crowd bowed in reverence to their life-giver.

"Hail, O great Ra!"

Mentuhotep, literally meaning Mentu is satisfied, continued as Hebrew slaves waved giant palm fronds to keep him cool in the searing heat.

"Mizris, just last year, the King of Lower Mizraim in Herakleopolis sent his army to desecrate our most sacred royal necropolis at Abydos. Since then, we have waged holy war against him, with the intention of uniting all of Mizraim and bringing together all of the lands of Egypt, to create the greatest empire the world has ever seen. May the death-chariot of Osiris sweep down on the Herakleopolitans at the head of my army marching north tomorrow and bring us a great victory. In triumph, I shall add the blue crown of Lower Mizraim to my white crown and together, United Mizraim shall rule all we survey."

Mentuhotep dropped a faux blue crown, signifying his enemy, and crushed it under his foot. The crowd roared with appreciation.

"Victory to Mentuhotep!"

On cue, a column of leather-breastplated and helmeted foot soldiers, led by the armour-plated General Suti in his war-chariot, paraded noisily into the square, armed to the teeth with swords, spears, bows and arrows. To boisterous cheering from the crowds, throwing garlands of flowers, General Suti led the Army of Upper Mizraim through the main square of Thebes towards the North Portal of the city. Geographically, Upper Mizraim lay south of Lower Mizraim, the divided states of the lands of Ancient Egypt.

Mentuhotep led the royal entourage back inside the sumptuous palace, where a gigantic banquet was laid out in the great hall in honour of Montu, the falcon-headed god of war. Vast quantities of food, wine and Egyptian mead were consumed in anticipation of a decisive victory on the battlefield.

Chapter 3

The parade of the Army of Upper Mizraim led by his top General Suti was arranged by Mentuhotep purely for show to pump up the crowd. After exiting the North Portal of Thebes, the troops only marched two kilometres north along the Nile on the road to Koptos, followed by a cohort of adoring Theban boys, play fighting with sticks for swords. As evening fell, Suti sent the boys back to the city and then ordered his officers to get the men to pitch camp for the night. Tents were erected off-road on the scrubland edging the eastern desert and the soldiers lit their campfires and began cooking their evening meals and drinking their beers.

By Pharaoh's invitation, Suti and his two most senior Lieutenant Commanders, Pawura and Nekhebet, rode on horseback to Thebes to join the riotous feasting in the palace. Suti was never one to miss a good party. Achillas, one of the many Greatest of Fifty commanders, sat eating a lamb and bean stew with his company and watched carefully as the senior officers rode back to Thebes. After finishing his meal and flagon of mead, he excused himself, winking.

"Hey, lads, I'm just going over the dunes for a shit. Here's hoping the scorpions aren't stinging this evening, eh?"

As he left the campfire, one of his men shouted after him.

"The scorpions wouldn't dare nip your pretty arse, Achi!"

Achillas was renowned for his agility in sport and his prowess in battle, but his men also admired him for his dashing good looks. They joked behind his back.

"Achillas might be able to pass his shit, but he can't pass a mirror."

Once over the tall dunes and out of sight of the camp, Achillas quickly turned south, cutting back towards the Theban road. Ra, the sun-god, had set on the other side of the Nile, below the far-off hills of the Sahara desert and it would soon be dark. The road was empty of travellers and Achillas broke into a trot, heading back towards Thebes.

By the time he neared the city walls, the sky was pitch black, except for the myriad of stars that brightened the Egyptian sky. Just above the horizon, Achillas made out the blinking planet of Horus the Red, the red traveller, rising in the night sky. He sent up a silent prayer.

"Horus, fiery god of war, protect me this night, from what I'm about to do."

When he reached the gates of the North Portal he tapped the handle of his sword on the smaller side gate. A Theban guard held a flaming torch to the grille and peered out.

"Who goes there?"

"I'm Achillas, a Greatest of Fifty. I've been sent with an important message for His Excellency, General Suti. I beg to enter the city walls."

The Theban guard relaxed and laughed.

"General Suti. He arrived a short while ago. He's at the palace with Mentu and they're all getting pissed. Lucky bastards."

Achillas heard the bolts being unlatched and the guard beckoned him in through the small side gate. Achillas thanked the guards on duty as he entered. They pointed along the street towards the main square.

"You know where the palace is. Straight up there."

He started to march purposefully up the street, when he was frozen by a cry from the guards.

"Hey, you!"

He turned his head slowly, trying not to show any fear. However, they were laughing.

"Bring us back a coupla legs of fried chicken, eh? And maybe a flagon of wine, if you can sneak it out."

Achillas gave them a dubious thumbs up and trotted on. Once around the bend in the street out of sight, he darted down narrow side-alleys, past the odd sleepy donkey, some squatting camels spitting at him and a screeching cat he almost tripped over. Eventually, he came along a wider alley, bringing him close to the rear of the Royal Palace. Pressing his muscular frame into the shadows, he hissed out a whisper, as loud as he dared.

"Iset!"

Nothing.

"Iset!"

A small, slender figure appeared from the direction of the palace building and drew close to him in the darkened alley-way. Achillas and Iset fell into each other's arms, kissing hungrily and embracing as if it was their last. He held her at arm's length and devoured her beauty, shining brightly, even in the darkness of the alley.

Iset, the youngest princess of Pharaoh Mentuhotep, was dressed in her finest party gear, her heavy make-up emphasising the beauty of her sparkling green almond-shaped eyes and her perfectly symmetrical face. She also bathed in the rugged, handsome features of her soldier-lover, with his high brow, square-set jaw and muscular build, dressed in his Greatest of Fifty army toga, his short sword sheathed on a thick leather belt around his firm waist.

"I can't stay away from my father's victory feast too long, Achi. Mentu pays me no attention and, anyway, the men are all pissed, but my mother keeps a beady eye on me."

"I know, Issi, I also need to get back to camp very soon, before one of my company reports me absent. We march north tomorrow to ensure your father wins his famous victory."

Iset bowed her head.

"I can't bear thinking you could die in battle, furthering the ambitions of my own father."

Achillas puffed up his broad frame, raising her delicate chin gently with his fingers.

"Hey, Issi, it'll take more than the Armies of Memphis and the Delta combined to bring down your beloved Achi. I'll be spending more time trying to keep old Suti alive, than worrying about myself."

Iset looked askance.

"God, I hate that Suti! The old drunken perv has been pawing over me all night. Says he wants to marry me. As if he hasn't got enough wives."

Achillas angered, clutching his sword.

"If Suti ever lays a finger on you! I swear Issi, I'll slice open his fat gizzard and leave him in the eastern desert for the buzzards."

"No, Achi, that won't solve anything."

"But I want us to be together forever, my love."

They embraced each other urgently.

"Don't worry, Issi. On the way here through the darkening desert, I sent a special prayer up to Horus the Red."

He pointed up to the little reddish blinking light of Mars and laughed.

"Horus, I said, send me your finest golden winged chariot and take Princess Iset and Greatest of Fifty commander Achillas up to the heavens, where they can love each other until eternity."

Iset laughed back.

"Oh, god, you're a dreamer, Achi. If only."

They were startled by a loud peal of laughter from the pillared cloisters at the palace rear. Two drunks were pawing all over a couple of giggling slave girls.

"Hell's teeth, that's my commanding officers, here with Suti."

"You must go, Achi, and I must return to the banquet, although, it'll break my heart."

They stole one last lingering kiss and as Iset moved back towards the palace, Achi called in a low voice.

"Issi, any chance of sneaking out some chicken and wine? It'll help me get past the guards at the North Portal."

Chapter 4

Bebi hurriedly waved in Nubian slaves carrying platters of ice-cold head-cloths and cool pitchers of water and beer. He ordered them to place the items on the low marble table in front of Mentuhotep. Pharaoh's Grand Vizier shooed the slaves out of the council room. Mentuhotep groaned, his forehead pressed on the cool marble.

"Mentu, wrap these cold compresses around your head."

"God sake, Bebi, I must have drunk for the whole of Thebes last night. What've you got for a hangover? Any of those vile potions of yours? Uurgh!"

Bebi poured a cup of beer and passed it to Pharaoh.

"Drink this, My Lord. It's the best hair-of-the-dog I know of. It's the strongest medicinal mead brewed by the female hand-maidens of the High Priests of Ur."

Mentuhotep sipped the sweet honey flavoured beer and straightened up.

"Talking about Ur, how's my new mausoleum coming on? The way I feel this morning, I might be needing it sooner, rather than later."

Bebi fiddled with a few papyri notes lying on the table and Mentuhotep tried vainly to squint a look at the hieroglyphs. He was seeing double and gave up.

"To be honest, Mentu, we've had to slow down the building works due to financial constraints. We've had to divert resources into your war-chest for the expansion of the Army of Upper Mizraim. Many of the slaves have been conscripted off the building site. However, when Suti returns victorious from battle and you unite all of Mizraim, there will be abundant treasures to construct an even larger mausoleum and the greatest pyramid ever built for any Pharaoh."

Mentuhotep thumped his fist on the table.

"Suti better come back with great victories and a huge treasure-chest. Y'know what? Last night, that fat, drunken old bastard had the cheek to ask for the hand of Princess Iset to add to his harem of haggard wives. She's barely…what age is she anyway?"

"Eighteen, sire."

"Yeah, eighteen. Well, I'm not having that old lecher slobbering over my youngest, most beautiful daughter. Send a message to him, tell him I'm offering him the hand of Princess Meketaten. She's…"

"Thirty, sire."

"…thirty, that's right. Well, I know the poor girl's as ugly as sin, but she can still bear him some little generals for the army."

Bebi scribbled a note to send to Suti on a blank scrap of papyrus.

"Meketaten would make a good wife for Suti. She is not a bad-looking girl, sire. Admittedly, not as beautiful as Iset."

Mentuhotep drained his cup of mead and held it up for his vizier to refill it.

"Ah, yes. Iset. That reminds me. My wife, God knows *her* name, y'know, Iset's mother. Well she was banging on at me at breakfast. Couldn't touch a blasted thing, I was so hungover. What was I on about?"

"Iset?"

"Iset, that's the one. Trouble remembering all my bleeding offspring, there's so many of them. Sometimes envy those eunuch priests. No children to worry them into an early grave. Well then, Bebi, one of my concubines told me she'd heard Iset may have fallen for a…a commoner. Your nose is always to the grindstone, heard anything about it?"

The Grand Vizier deliberated on a diplomatic answer, fiddling again with the papyri.

"I've heard rumours, Mentu. There's talk amongst the slave girls that Iset's courting a low-ranked soldier in Suti's army."

"Do we know which soldier?"

"No name as such. I believe from the girls his tunic bore the insignia of a Greatest of Fifty commander. Suti has a great many soldiers of that rank."

"I assume this soldier will be marching north today?"

"Of course, Mentu."

"Bebi, send out your spies and find this soldier. He must be deployed in the forefront of every battle. Make sure he never gets the chance to march back to Thebes ever again. He can return as one of our glorious dead. Understand?"

"Understood, Pharaoh."

Chapter 5

The Vor-maga I Commander lay dozing in his bunk, when his intercom crackled. The ship's Chief Engineer asked to meet him at Hold 4 to discuss an emerging problem. The tired Commander made his way down immediately and the engineer was waiting for him.

"What's up, Chief?"

The engineer guided his Commander into Hold 4.

"The problem's up here, Commander. Deep-freeze silo 9. See the warning light indicator here?"

"Yes, what's that telling us?"

"It indicates there's a very slow leak of liquid nitrogen. My engineers and I have had a look and it is in an inaccessible and irreparable position."

The Commander shook his head.

"So, Chief, the DNA stockpiles in silo 9 are likely to be destroyed then?"

"Well, sir, we are talking many Vor-magan years before the DNA will be defrosted. However, we will all be going into deep-sleep in the cryogenic capsules for four, maybe five, Vor light years. The silo will definitely be defrosted by then and the DNA will be lost."

The Commander placed his hand on silo 9.

"What's your view then? Should we jettison the silo as it's just going to be dead-weight on our journey?"

The Chief shrugged.

"Yes, we could do that, Commander. However, there's another possible option."

"What's that?"

"Well, sir, we'll reach the blue traveller in a quarter Vor-magan year, with miniscule leakage from silo 9. While you are carrying out your research on the sub-Bor-aks, my engineers and I propose to seal-wrap the silo. We can transport it down to the planet's frozen southern land and bury the silo deep under the ice. Hopefully, one day our descendants can return and so reclaim the DNA if and when required."

"Hmm, is it a big job?"

"It's a tricky operation, sir, but it's doable. If you will authorise me a robotic craft, I believe we can safely transfer the silo down to the icy southern land."

"Okay, Chief, I'll authorise the operation. Keep an eye on the silo and we'll make a final decision once we're in the blue traveller's orbit."

Chapter 6

The day's dust-filled march north on the road to Koptos had begun in a blazing sun and the great caravan of the Army of Upper Mizraim writhed its way snake-like parallel to the great winding Nile. Scores of villagers, artisans and farmers rushed to the roadside to cheer the troops as they marched through.

"Give Memphis hell!"

"Smite the enemy!"

The soldiers waved back cheerily and accepted floral garlands around their necks and kisses from pretty young girls. Greatest of Fifty commander Achillas marched at the head of his company, alongside his comrade in arms, Corporal Mesehti.

"Where'd you get to last night, Achi? Off humping some young thing no doubt."

"Leave it out, Mesi. I did meet someone last night, but I love her with all my heart."

Mesehti swivelled his head from side to side rolling his eyes in disbelief at what he was hearing.

"Achillas is in *love*? I don't believe it! The man who could shag any girl in the whole of Upper Mizraim has fallen in love."

"Oh, give it a rest, Mesi."

Mesehti looked back to the company and spoke out the side of his mouth.

"Hey, boys, Achi here has fallen in love. This one must be nothing less than a princess. Nothing's too good for our Achi."

The soldiers marching immediately behind burst into laughter.

"Forget it, Mesi. Anyway, she *is* too good for me and the likelihood is I'll never see her again. I'll be dead and butchered on some bloody field of Mizraim."

"Huh, no chance. The rest of us will likely be skewered, but not our gorgeous Achillas. You're indestructible. You'll live forever."

"I'm no blooming god, Mesi. Let's just get to Koptos for the night. C'mon, give us one of your famous marching songs."

Mesehti was a travelling actor and singer in civvy life and it took no encouragement for him to start singing.

"Come away the lads of Mizraim.
Let's march along to our Theban hymn.
Let all our enemies retreat in fear.
When they see the gallant Mizris here."

It was a well-known camp song and one company after another started marching to the Theban hymn. The bold singing rippled its way along the line to the front, where General Suti led the marching troops, mounted on his trusty grey charger. His war-chariot had been dismantled and packed in one of the wagons at the back of the caravan train. Lieutenant Commander Pawura rode beside Suti.

"The lads are in good cheer, General. Augers well for the battlefield."

Like Mentuhotep, Suti was nursing a hangover.

"Huh, let's hope they're all still singing after we clash with the Armies of Memphis and the Delta. It will be a bloody gore-fest, no doubt."

Pawura, who had refrained from over-indulging at the banquet, remained in an optimistic mood. He and Lieutenant Commander Nekhebet had preferred enjoying the pleasures of two feisty Babylonian slave girls at the palace rear instead.

"General, you've probably assembled the greatest army ever seen in all of Egypt. Memphis won't know what's hit him."

"Hmm, Pawura, you know full well a general never agrees he's enough resources to face his enemies. It's been years since we've fought any great battles against Lower Mizraim and our intelligence on Memphis and the Delta is sorely lacking. We need to know their troop sizes and movements."

Pawura agreed and Suti continued.

"Order Lieutenant Nekhebet to take the Camel Corps ahead of us up through the eastern desert parallel to the Red Sea.

Tell him to obtain intelligence on any enemy troop movements. Nekhebet can re-join us either in Qau or further north in Badari in a week or so."

"Yes, sir!"

Pawura swung his horse around and rode off to find Nekhebet.

As he rode back down the line, the singing was abruptly interrupted from the rear. He could see a rider coming along the Koptos road towards him and the troops were distracted by the passing horseman. As he rode past, some wag shouted out to a burst of laughter and cheers.

"Is the war all over then?"

The rider pulled up beside Lieutenant Pawura.

"General Suti? Message from the palace."

Pawura pointed back.

"He's the fat guy leading the parade."

The rider galloped ahead, as Pawura continued his search for Nekhebet. Suti turned to see what the fuss was, just as the messenger rode up beside him, beating his chest in salute.

"A message from Lord Mentu, Your Excellency."

The two riders pulled to the side of the road as the troop train rumbled past, marching northwards. Suti unrolled the sealed papyrus and read it. It contained two notes from Grand Vizier Bebi. The first stated Mentuhotep was sending his apology that Princess Iset was too young for marriage, but that Pharaoh gladly proffered the hand of his eldest daughter, the Princess Meketaten instead. The second papyrus note stated Mentu would be sending a couple of observers to join the march. Observers my arse, bloody spies, thought Suti. He reread the messages and cursed his luck under his breath. Politically, he could not turn down Pharaoh, but then again, he might die in battle, so c'est la vie.

"Will there be any message in return, General?"

Suti exhaled a deep sigh.

"Tell Bebi - the answer is yes to both."

Chapter 7

The Chief Engineer arrived on the bridge, after a call from the Commander.

"Reporting on bridge as ordered, sir."

The Commander motioned for them to sit privately at the council table away from the other crew who continued to monitor the computers, screens and instruments.

"I've been giving it some thought, following the leak in the DNA silo. I don't want any more glitches to jeopardise our long mission out into the galaxy. We are the last vestige of hope of the Bor-ak race, Chief."

"Affirmative, Commander, what d'you have in mind?"

"The initial program plan states, when we pass through the Great Asteroid Belt on the outer edge of the Vor system and into deep space, we will all simultaneously enter the cryogenic capsules. We'll be frozen for many Vor light years."

"That's the plan, sir, is it a problem?"

"I hope not, but I want to do a short-run test of the cryogenic capsules, while we're still in the Vor system. Find two volunteers, one male, one female, and we'll cryogenically freeze them from now until we enter blue traveller orbit."

The Chief nodded.

"Leave it with me, sir. I'll get two healthy specimens. It'll be a valid system test."

Chapter 8

Nekhebet's Camel Corps were encamped at an oasis about fifteen kilometres north east of Koptos, with the corps pushing well forward of Suti's main troop train along the Nile. For all intents and purposes, they could easily pass for a caravan of nomadic merchants heading north from the port of Quseir on the Red Sea. Although, if captured, under intense interrogation, that ruse would not hold much water, so it was vital to remain undetected by the enemy.

A welcome cooling breeze was blowing from the east off the Red Sea through Nekhebet's tent, as he sat lunching with his Corps Captain. Two days ago, he had dispatched three of his most experienced desert scouts due north on a reconnaissance operation and he was expecting them back soon.

"Well, Cap'n, you got big plans for when this fucking campaign's finished?"

The Captain mulled the question over.

"First things first, Nekhi, is to get out of this damned war in one piece. I've served Pharaoh's army nearly fifteen years and I'm planning to retire. I've a small family farm on the Wadi Mammamat, a few kilometres from Koptos. Just looking for a quiet life."

Nekhebet munched some juicy grapes and nodded in agreement.

"Sounds great. Although, I've a good few years to go yet before I can think of my pension. When I get back, I hope to make a good political marriage."

"Got someone in mind, Nekhi?"

"Princess Iset."

The Captain let out a whistle and Nekhebet continued.

"Have you ever seen her, Cap'n? By Ra, she's gorgeous. I spotted her sneaking back into the palace when Pawura and I were canoodling a coupla Babylonian slaves. You've never seen anything so beautiful."

"Rumour is Suti has his eye on her too, sir. That's mighty stiff competition."

Nekhebet nodded.

"I've heard that too. You'd think the old bugger has had his fill of wives and concubines. Well, if both of us make it back to Thebes alive, let the best man win…"

They were interrupted by loud voices outside the tent. The duty corporal popped his head in the open awning.

"Sir, recce scouts have arrived back. The officer's here with his report."

Nekhebet beckoned the officer in. A world-weary, dust-covered and unshaven camel corpsman blustered into the tent. Nekhebet pointed to the ample food on the low table and the officer lay down and grabbed some cold chicken legs. Nekhebet and the Captain both wrinkled their noses at the awful smell.

"God sake, you smell like the hind end of a dead camel!"

The corpsman shrugged, spluttering a mixture of cold chicken and wine as he spoke.

"Sorry, sir, we just got back five minutes ago. Not had time for a dip in the oasis yet. Thought you'd want our report ASAP."

"Yes, yes, man, let's have it then."

The corpsman helped himself to more chicken and tucked a bunch of grapes into his tunic.

"For later, sir. Getting to my report. Out on recce we managed to ride about sixty kilometres north. The eastern desert was as empty as a starving vulture's stomach until we were about ten kilometres south of the Hurghada oasis."

He paused for effect and another munch at his chicken leg. The Captain responded.

"Then what?"

"We were reconnoitring in a wadi while our camels drank water and we espied a small camel corps, definitely enemy, out scouting. Obviously, doing the same as us."

Nekhebet's eyes narrowed.

"Then the northern army must be on the move."

The corpsman agreed.

"No doubt about it, sir. We could make out a large dust cloud rising about thirty to forty kilometres to the north-west of Hurghada. My guess, about halfway between Herakleopolis and Beni Hasan. Not a breath of wind to stir up dust."

"The enemy army marching south. Did the enemy scouts spot you?"

The corpsman shook his head.

"Not as far as I could tell. We scarpered back here right away."

Nekhebet was pleased.

"Good work, corpsman. Go and get that wash now. Oh, and help yourself to whatever you can carry as a thanks to you and your comrades."

The corpsman smiled broadly, taking as much food and wine as he could carry in his broad arms and swiftly exited the tent. The Captain whistled again.

"We've a battle coming soon, Nekhi?"

"My guess is we'll collide somewhere between Asyut and Amarna, probably in a week or so...Right, Cap'n, get the order out to pack the corps up. We'll move out in the morning and meet up with Suti somewhere between Qau and Badari. The bloody war is here at last!"

Chapter 9

Suti's army marched into Abydos to a hero's welcome. The Abydosian citizens had suffered terribly when the King of Herakleopolis sacked their sacred royal necropolis and ordered rape and pillage throughout the city. Many unarmed civilians were murdered and Suti's arrival was seen as the ultimate act of vengeance to smite Lower Mizraim. Palm-waving crowds loudly greeted the Army of Upper Mizraim.

"Death to Memphis and the Delta!"

"Avenge our fathers and mothers!"

The weary army encamped on the northern outskirts of Abydos, close to where the necropolis was being restored. There was an urgency to erect tents and campfires. It was obvious a large thunderstorm was moving in off the Sahara from the west. It would be a very wet night, but Suti saw that as good tidings, so long as the summer storm moved through quickly.

His army could march tomorrow to Akhim and the following day on to Qau and they would not have dusty roads to tramp on. This would make marching more comfortable for his men, but more importantly, there would be no dust clouds to give away his position to Memphis and the Delta. Just as the first heavy plops of rain spattered the roof of the General's tent, a guard informed him two riders had arrived from Thebes.

Suti and the two spies sat in camp seats with some wine and the general began.

"Well then, gentlemen, what is the latest pleasure that Mentu has bestowed on me. Don't tell me he's found me an even uglier wife?"

The spies looked at each other, quite bewildered. The senior spy replied.

"No, General Suti, we're here on a different mission from Pharaoh..."

He was interrupted by the first flash of lightning, then

followed quickly by a loud crack of thunder. The ancients always saw a thunderstorm as a portent of evil, a message from the gods of the underworld. The senior spy shivered superstitiously.

"…Our mission's to find and seek out one of your junior ranks. He's been acting inappropriately towards Princess Iset."

Suti's eyebrows arched in surprise.

"Princess Iset? Give me the man's name and I'll have him hung, drawn and quartered in the morning!"

The senior spy raised his palm.

"Firstly, sir, we don't know his name and it's obvious, neither do you. Secondly, we've orders from Mentu that we mustn't touch this soldier. Mentu doesn't want Iset to blame her father for the death of her lover."

Another thunderclap roared across the heavens and rain poured down on the tent.

"By Osiris, you're saying Iset loves a lowly soldier in my army, when she could have the likes of me. I'll kill the bastard myself!"

"General, Mentu's orders are to ensure this man dies a heroic death in battle. Pharaoh will graciously honour him with a full military funeral with all the honours of Lower Mizraim bestowed on him. He feels this will appease Iset and not attach blame directly on him."

Suti growled unhappily.

"I don't follow Mentu's logic, but an order's an order. However, I've over ten thousand men camped out there. How do we find lover-boy without a name?"

The junior spy chipped in.

"How many Greatest of Fifty men do you have?"

Another loud bang exploded in the heavens and the rain intensified.

"Greatest of Fifty? Is that his rank?"

"Yes, sir."

Suti shuffled through his papyri in his travelling war-chest and pulled out a list of his army by rank and numbers.

"Let me see, Greatest of Fifty. Ah yes, currently I've one hundred and sixty three men of that rank. Actually, well short of complement, due to the rush to start this campaign. I've a few promotions to effect in the next couple of days. But I digress, 163 is still a big number to whittle down to one. We could be on the battlefield within a week."

The senior spy agreed.

"It's bigger than we'd hoped for, but we are experts in our field. We'll find him and soon. What can you give us in terms of the Greatest of Fifty details?"

"My aide-de-camp can provide you in the morning with the names, ages, length of service and marital status of all 163 men."

Another roar of thunder boomed out in the night.

"Excellent, General Suti. Our man is most likely to be one of the younger unmarried soldiers, so we should pin him down pretty quickly."

Chapter 10

Across the other side of the encampment, where the tents were not as waterproof as General Suti's, there was an incessant drip-drip-drip of rainwater into various jugs and beakers in the tent of Achillas, Mesehti and two other ranks. The fierce thunderstorm crashed violently overhead unabated. With every lightning flash, Mesehti flinched in fear.

"God sake, Achi, if there's one thing I hate, it's thunder and lightning. It never bodes well for the future."

Achillas laughed with disdain.

"Augh, Mesi, calm down. It's just part of nature. I don't believe in all your superstitious hocus-pocus."

"I'm telling you, Achi, my late father was a seer. He could foretell the future and he told me thunderstorms always carried a message from the gods. He told me I've inherited a bit of his second-sight."

"Okay, Mesi the seer, so what signs are the gods sending you tonight."

The thunder was slowing in intensity, with the lightning flashes moving east towards the Red Sea. Mesehti relaxed a little. He picked up a beaker almost full of rainwater and he quickly spilled a few drops on the sandy floor of the tent. The four men watched mesmerised as the water found its own paths, forming a spidery-shaped puddle. Mesehti stared intently at the watery shape, then closed his eyes in meditation, holding up his palm for silence. The atmosphere in the tent became thick and palpable.

"Well? What vision sendeth the gods, O Great Seer?"

Mesehti stared weirdly at Achillas.

"I...I don't like it, Achi."

"Like what, Mesi, c'mon, what do your thunder-gods tell you? Spit it out."

One of the others cracked a joke.

"Don't tell us, Pharaoh's going to ban mirrors and poor

old Achi won't be able to admire his reflection."

Mesehti shook his head dolefully.

"No, if only. The gods are sending two signs. Firstly, Achi will be promoted in the field..."

Achillas laughed.

"Hey, Mesi, that's good news, why the long face?"

"The promotion's not good news. It's designed to get you killed on the battlefront."

"And do I get killed? Me, Achi the indestructible!"

Mesehti stared again at the puddle.

"I can't say, Achi, but look at the puddle. What does it look like?"

"I don't know, Mesi, let's say...a spider."

"Not bad. But what does the spider have here?"

Mesehti pointed to the back of the spidery puddle and Achillas pondered for a moment.

"Oh, I see it. The spider's got a long curving tail, so..."

"So, Achillas, it's not a spider, it's a scorpion."

"Oh, I get it now, Mesi. I'm going to be promoted, but then I'm going to be killed on the battlefield by a giant armoured scorpion ridden aloft by the King of Memphis."

Achillas and the other two soldiers laughed heartily. The thunderstorm had passed and the stillness following a North African desert storm descended over the camp. They all felt the uplifting change in atmospheric pressure.

"No, Achi, the gods will take the body of the sleeping warrior Achillas up to the heavens, not killed by a giant scorpion, but driven on a silver chariot towards the giant scorpion."

The tent went silent.

Then, Achillas slapped Mesehti's back, as they all burst into laughter.

"What a load of absolute bollocks, Mesi, old pal."

Chapter 11

Mentuhotep sat impatiently on his lesser throne, losing his cool, as two black topless Nubian slave girls fanned him. He called for his Grand Vizier.

"Bebi! What's keeping you?"

Bebi came rushing in to the lesser throne room, his bare feet slipping on the polished marble, then regaining his balance with his was-sceptre, his long staff of office.

"Princess Iset and her mother will be here momentarily, Mentu. Something of a make-up crisis held them up, I believe."

Mentuhotep raised his arms to the heavens.

"Make-up crisis? I don't give a fig about make-up. When Pharaoh commands an audience before him, Mentu expects punctuality. Bebi, you will be..."

He was halted mid-sentence as the vision of beauty that was his daughter Iset strolled regally into the room, with her mother slightly cowering behind. It had been a while since he had slept with this wife, but Mentuhotep thought, *hey, I'd forgotten what a looker she was. I see where Iset gets her beauty from.*

He changed his tack and reworded his command to Bebi.

"As I was saying, Bebi, you will be...taking the Nubians out and giving me a moment with my family."

Bebi clapped loudly and he led the slave girls out to the ante-room. Mentuhotep signalled for the women to relax on the floor before his golden throne. His wife prostrated herself in adoration before her Pharaoh. Iset stretched out haughtily below her father, her pristine white low-cut shift giving him a bird's-eye view of her perfect décolletage. His brow beaded with sweat. *My god,* he thought, *if she weren't my daughter, I'd take her for my own wife.* The ancient god-kings of Mizraim were not averse to incest in the past, but it was a step too far for Mentuhotep.

"Wife, sit up and let me see you. It's been a while."

She raised herself on her knees and he was pleased at the sight. Iset was less than pleased to be there and began very sarcastically.

"Well, father, you wished to see us. Not often we get the pleasure of your esteemed company."

The Nubian girls quickly and quietly re-entered the room, laying down small silver platters full of traditional Mizri sweetmeats, exiting just as quickly.

"Iset, my beautiful princess, don't be angry with me. Try some of these goodies on offer. Wife, pass me some."

Iset's mother crawled forward on her knees, her head bowed and raised a platter for Mentuhotep to select some sweetmeats.

"Mm, these honeyed almonds are delicious. Won't you try some, Iset?"

"I've had my breakfast, thank you, Pharaoh. I'm sure you wouldn't want me to spoil my hour-glass figure and thus displease my new husband, that fat old bastard, General Suti!"

Her mother hissed out of the side of her mouth.

"Iset! Respect your god-king."

Mentuhotep laughed it off dismissively.

"Hah, is that what you think of your father? That he would marry you off to old Suti. Well, you're wrong. You're far too young for the old lecher. Instead, he's agreed to marry your sister Princess…um…Princess Meketaten. She'll make a good match and provide me with little generals."

Iset was relieved for herself, but horrified for her sister.

"Meketaten with Suti? That's obscene. Has she agreed to this? Mother, have you?"

Pharaoh banged his sceptre angrily on the arm of the throne.

"Enough of this insolence, Iset. I personally intervened with Suti on your behalf and he will marry Meketaten. That's the end of the matter."

"And what of me, Pharaoh? Am I to be denied a chance

of love?"

"Iset, only a High Prince of the Mizris will be good enough for my princess. Bebi is trawling through suitors as we speak. But, you're only…only…"

His wife spoke.

"Only eighteen, my Lord."

"Of course, eighteen. Still plenty time for me to find you a suitable husband you can love."

Tears welled up in Iset's heavily-mascaraed eyes.

"What if I want to love a man for the sake of love itself?"

Her mother was horrified. Mentuhotep angrily leaned forward.

"Issi, don't think your father's blind. He knows what's going on behind his back and it stops right here! You will love whoever Pharaoh commands you to love. No common soldier will be a son-in-law at the court of Mentuhotep. Is that clear?"

Iset's mother intervened.

"What are you talking about, Pharaoh?"

He stood tall before Iset, pointed his was-sceptre at her, and roared.

"She knows full well what I'm talking about. But then Pharaoh is all-seeing."

Iset wept bitterly into her hands, as her confused mother tried to console her.

"I…I love him…with all my heart."

"Love who? What's his name?"

Iset realised Pharaoh was not quite as all-seeing as he made out.

"I'll never betray him!"

Mentuhotep sneered.

"Young bloody love. You're carrying a torch for some poor lad who's likely to die needlessly for King and country. Look, Iset, I'm taking the Royal Barge down the Nile tomorrow. Off to review Suti's army before his great battle. If you give me the lad's name, I'll arrange an honourable discharge for him. You can let him live, just not in Thebes?"

"Never! He would never forgive me. He's the bravest man I've ever known. He doesn't know what you're like, as I do, but he will lay down his life for you."

Iset shrugged her mother off and ran out of the throne room weeping for her poor Achillas. Her mother looked pleadingly at Mentuhotep.

"Mentu, she'll get over him. You find her a prince and I'll work on Iset. I'll also prepare Meketaten for marriage."

"Wife, you have pleased me with your words. It's been a while, but I'm pleasantly surprised. You've looked after yourself. Come to my bed chamber tonight. You can pleasure me before my trip tomorrow."

Iset's mother groaned inwardly.

"Yes, Pharaoh."

Chapter 12

The Navigator carefully eased the Vor-maga I into a high planetary geosynchronous orbit. The huge craft orbited the blue planet in a fixed position directly above the equatorial African continent. The large screens had a bird's-eye view of mankind's known world of the ancients. The Navigator relayed the situation to the Commander.

"Vor-maga I safely in fixed orbit, sir."

"Good work, Navigator."

He viewed the screen in front of him, observing the beautiful bejewelled blue planet far below his mothership. A tear formed reminiscing on an old memory.

"It's beautiful and so full of life, just as our own beloved red traveller once was. It's such a pity the blue traveller's gravity would crush us alive."

"Yes, sir. Let's hope one day we discover our own new red traveller."

"I'm sure we will, Navigator. Carry on, I'm leaving the bridge to meet the Chief Engineer on the cryogenic deck. Keep monitoring our orbital position and call me immediately if you have any problems."

*

The Chief Engineer saluted as the Commander entered the chilled cryogenic deck. The Ship's Doctor was also on deck and attending to his instrument panels. The Commander glanced at the panels.

"Gentlemen, how's our two brave volunteers doing?"

The Doctor replied.

"They're both in the final stages of thawing out. So far, vital signs are excellent and they've coped extremely well in deep hibernation. The tricky bit is when their hearts are shocked back to normal rhythms by the system. Any minute now."

The three Bor-ak officers shuffled over to observe both

capsules one and two. The male and female volunteers appeared to be sleeping peacefully. A green light flashed on the panel of capsule one and the female's body jolted with the defibrillating electric shock. The Commander looked dubiously at the Doctor, but he smiled reassuringly.

"It's painless, sir. She feels nothing."

The green light flashed on capsule two and the Bo-rak male received his electric shock. Gradually, the volunteers' eyes flickered open and they stared bemusedly at the three officers. The Doctor entered codes on the capsules' panels and they flicked open with a whoosh due to the pressure change. The Doctor questioned his patients.

"How are you both feeling?"

"Hungry."

"Thirsty."

The Doctor turned to the Commander.

"Everything's normal, sir. I think we've just had a very successful test run."

"Well done, Doctor. Carry on."

The Commander led the Chief Engineer back out into the corridor.

"That test went well, Chief. Looks like the cryogenic capsules will do the job."

"Definitely, sir. I'd suggest doing a repeat test with some more volunteers. Say, whilst we remain in blue traveller orbit, then do the slingshot around Vor and re-awaken them part-way through the Vor system."

"Affirmative, Chief. Best to be doubly sure."

"I'll make arrangements, sir."

"Now, Chief, what about the plan for Deep-freeze silo 9?"

"I've readied a landing ship and AI robotic crew. All I need is your agreement for my engineering team to disconnect the silo and transport it to the frozen southern land. We'll seal-wrap it, drill a core and bury it with a long-range tracking device deep in the ice."

The Commander sought further reassurance.

"Is this operation worth the risk, Chief?"

"In my view, it's worth doing, sir. The liquid nitrogen level's still at 97%. By burying it deep in the ice core, it should remain in perpetuity, until our descendants can return to reclaim the DNA material."

"Okay, commence Operation Deep-freeze. I'll now get started on observing our little sub-Bor-ak friends and see what they're up to."

Chapter 13

Bebi's two spies sat in a cramped tent provided by Suti, poring over the papyri lists. The army was now camped three kilometres south of Badari and close to the Upper-Lower border. Nekhebet's Camel Corps had returned from their recce in the eastern desert and reported back to the General. Rumours were rife throughout camp the enemy was somewhere near Amarna, just twenty-five kilometres to the north. Battle fever was rife. The senior spy held up his papyrus note.

"We've kinda whittled it down to these five Greatest of Fifty. But, with the battle looking imminent, I'd like to pin this guy down tomorrow and get the hell back to Thebes."

"Yeah, me too. I certainly didn't sign up for any of the fighting."

"Okay, what's your gut feeling?"

The junior spy looked at the five names.

"I've spent the afternoon digging into the backgrounds of the five of them."

"What have you found?"

The junior pointed to his senior's list.

"The first man, I'd definitely rule him out. Prefers men from what I've heard. This second, he's unmarried, but very doubtful he'll ever wed."

"Oh, why?"

"Severely injured his manhood in a gladiatorial fight. Not princess material, unless she fancies a semi-eunuch."

The senior inked red dots beside one and two.

"Now, number four's a possible, but I don't favour him. He's a fine specimen of manhood, but he's Nubian. A black ex-slave, gained his freeman papyri by working his way up in the army. Seems a step too far for a Mizri princess."

Another red dot and then the senior looked up.

"That leaves three and five. What's the story there?"

"Both men certainly fit the bill. Tall, muscular, athletic soldiers. Type of men who could easily turn a pretty young girl's head. Both single, but…"

"But what?"

"Rumour has it number five has a lovely fiancée back in Thebes. Apparently getting married after the war's over."

"What about number three, then? What's your gut?"

"I fancy him as our main target. I've talked to quite a few soldiers who know him well. He's admired by all his men, a great man-manager and commands respect. And he has the reputation for being the best-looking guy in the whole army. He'd definitely see himself as princess material."

"So, number five…red dot. And… number three…the Greatest of Fifty Achillas…blue dot?"

The junior spy nodded enthusiastically.

"Okay, so find out all you can on Achillas and then we'll report back to General Suti tomorrow."

Chapter 14

Mentuhotep's fleet of three barges was making steady progress down the Nile and his Royal Barge would dock at Badari in the morning. A dispatch rider had been dropped off at Qau to ride ahead and relay the message for Suti, Pawura and Nekhebet to report aboard the next day for a war council. Mentu and Bebi sat under the large awning drinking fine wine in the evening air, listening to the solemn drumbeat and cracking of whips keeping the slave oarsmen concentrated on their task. They enjoyed the splash and plop caused by the sailors on the bow sounding the depth of the Nile.

There was a cool breeze blowing across a cloudless star-filled sky. Every now and then, they spotted the odd falling star flash its small, bright fiery trail high above.

"The gods are travelling in the heavens tonight, Bebi."

The Grand Vizier was half-drunk on the strong wine, but assumed Pharaoh required some prophetic reply.

"They know war's coming, sire, and they're taking their seats in the ethereal grandstands above us, tossing their dice and betting on the victor."

"And are all the safe bets placed on Mentu's army?"

Bebi hiccupped drunkenly. No great prophetic visions appeared to him, so a fib would have to suffice.

"With Ra, Osiris and Montu on Pharaoh's side, victory for Suti is guaranteed."

*

Ahead of the Royal Barge was the lead barge carrying the Pharaonic guards. It was well lit and making good progress down the Nile. On the supply barge taking up the rear, the oarsmen were struggling to keep pace. All the strongest slaves were chosen for the lead barge and the Royal Barge. The tired slaves aboard the supply barge were receiving a heavy dose of the lash. However, the Captain of the Whip was tough, but fair. Some of the slaves had been working the oars for over three hours and it was time for a shift change.

A line of fresh oarsmen were drawn up from below deck. The Captain pointed each slave into position, relieving an exhausted rower. Working his way towards the stern, he spotted a slight figure on one of the rear starboard oars. The young lad was definitely struggling with exhaustion, his hands bandaged, blistered and bloodied. The officer appointed a replacement to take his oar. The lad struggled to his feet and the officer was taken aback by his lack of height and frame.

"You lad, what age are you?"

Iset lied.

"Fourteen, sir."

"Fourteen? Still a small 'un for a lad o' fourteen. How'd you get on my oar crew?"

Iset's legs wobbled unsteadily.

"Ran away from home, sir, off to join Suti's army."

Iset did not hear the howls of laughter as she collapsed on the wooden deck. A couple of slaves were ordered to carry Iset down below to recover. Fortunately, for the young princess, they did not inspect her too closely and assumed she was a small boy who had become over-exhausted at the oar.

*

Back on the Royal Barge, Bebi was half-asleep and he was mumbling drunken nonsense. Mentuhotep was still having his wine cup refilled by a very attractive Hebrew slave named Ruth. The raven-haired girl flashed an endearingly shy smile each time she filled his cup. Mentu had been fully satisfied last night by his wife, but, *could I*, he wondered. Before he returned her smile, his eye glimpsed the North Star over the girl's shoulder. It looked too bright. Then he realised the North Star was moving.

"Bebi, what's that in the heavens?"

"Eh?"

Mentuhotep sharply elbowed Bebi's arm and pointed northwards. A huge fireball with a tail of light arced its way south across the Sahara, leaving behind a distinct vapour trail. The two men stared in awe and the Hebrew girl Ruth collapsed in fear as the gigantic shooting star passed overhead. It soon disappeared below the southern horizon. Another slave helped the shaking girl to her feet and took her below deck. Bebi tried to make sense of the phenomenon.

"A fiery chariot of the gods, My Lord."

"And what was it prophesying?"

"I'm sure…a great victory for Mentu."

"Oh yeah, then why was it going in the total opposite direction of the battlefield?"

Bebi had no answer to this conundrum.

Chapter 15

The Bor-ak spaceship landed safely on the icy surface of the great southern land in the black of night. It was the summer season of Shemu when it passed over Egypt, but at the South Pole it was entering the winter season of Peret. Vor did not rise and fall and only a faint half-light emerged during the day. Dark and light was of no consequence to the AI robots crewing the ship, but their first task was to erect a large circle of arc lights around the ship and the drilling site. This was to allow visual transmission back to Vor-maga I's on board satellite via a fixed-position beacon orbiting above the south pole.

The AI robots were large and cumbersome on the blue traveller, originally designed for the lower gravity of their red traveller. The thick snow and ice was also an added hindrance. However, they were sturdy enough to cope with the increased pressures exerted by the stronger gravitational field. The Vor-maga Operator on the satellite's hi-res camera monitor relayed a SitRep to the Commander and the engineering team sitting at the council table.

"The core drilling machine has been positioned by the robots on site and is ready to commence operation, sir."

The Commander turned to his Chief Engineer.

"Drilling engineer good to go?"

"Yes, Commander."

"Okay, activate deep drill."

The Chief Engineer commanded the drilling engineer to commence operations and the Operator updated the SitRep.

"Drilling of the ice core has commenced successfully, sir."

The operation would take the best part of a day. They needed to drill out the core sections, each section of ice being set aside by the AI robots. Once the deep core had been drilled to the required depth, the seal-wrapped Deep-freeze silo 9 would be lowered into the ice shaft, followed by replacing the ice sections until the core was refilled. The robots would pack all the heavy equipment back on board for their craft's return to the mothership.

The Commander dismissed the other engineers at the table and sat alone with the Chief.

"Everything's running smoothly, Chief."

"Looks like we've saved that DNA for the future, sir."

The Commander agreed the operation was worth the risk, then changed the subject.

"I've been monitoring the little sub-Bor-aks in the region directly below us."

"Have they advanced over the 4,000 Vor-magan years since our ancestors last visited?"

"In many ways they have, Chief. They're the only hominid sub-species we selected for transmutation to survive, mainly due to their ability to embrace technological advances in the use of tools and equipment, and advances in collective agricultural and manufacturing techniques."

"That's very encouraging, sir. If we don't survive the journey across the galaxy, at least we know our Bor-ak genes will survive in some form."

"Very true, Chief. However, their advances are now showing the downsides that our own ancestors possessed many millennia past."

The Commander displayed satellite photos of the two armies massing close to the border between the two Mizri states.

"They've developed into factional warrior tribes of city states led by hierarchical leaders and, as you can see here, two of these tribes are squaring up for a great battle. We Bor-ak also developed advanced military technologies in the past, threatening to completely destroy ourselves. But we learned to tread the path of peace."

"Should we intervene in this battle, Commander?"

"No, our orders are merely to observe the sub-Bor-ak,

ascertain the continued future of our gene pool is assured and to deliver a specific message from our planet to a key sub-Bor-ak leader."

"A message, sir?"

The Commander punched a code on the table and the top slid open, revealing a flat slab of red arenite sandstone from the Western Arabia Terra region from the red planet, carved in Bor-ak. The Chief read the intricately carved rock.

The last of the great beings of the red traveller sowed his seed among the beings of the blue traveller. Many seeds failed. One seed thrived and then there was the new being.

"A bit cryptic, sir?"

"The sub-Bora-aks are still fairly primitive beings, however, I will explain the message in greater detail to the chosen sub-Bor-ak leader in person."

"In person? But you can't go down to the blue traveller. You'd die, sir."

"I know that, but, once the Silo 9 mission is finished, we can use the robot-crewed ship to bring the sub-Bor-ak leader up here!"

Chapter 16

Around noon, the war council was assembled aboard the upper deck of the great Royal Barge at the port of Badari. Mentuhotep, wearing his white crown, sat under the awning on a golden-painted wooden throne at the head of the low feast-laden table. Bebi sat beside the throne with his pen and papyri at the ready. General Suti, Lieutenant Commanders Pawura and Nekhebet lay stretched out around the tempting food and wine. Pharaoh pointed his was-sceptre at the feast.

"Tuck in, men, as I always say, Pharoah's army never marches on an empty stomach."

The food and wine began to flow and tongues began to loosen.

"So Suti, what news of the enemy? Have we a fight on our hands?"

The General tried to quickly swallow a mouthful of food before addressing Mentuhotep.

"My Lord, we plan to attack the Armies of Memphis and the Delta in two days from hence. The enemy has taken up a defensive line on the border between our city of Asyut and their city of Amarna to the north."

"Excellent, General. May the falcon-head of Montu lead you onto victory? So what's your strategy?"

Suti shoved some of the plates aside and laid a simple papyrus map on the table before Mentuhotep.

"Here is our army at Badari and tomorrow we march to Asyut in preparation for the attack. Here is the defensive line of the Memphis and the Delta on the border. My main divisions of the Theban regiments will attack the Memphis divisions on our left flank and drive them into the Nile. Pawura's divisions, which include the regiments of Heirakonpolis, Koptos, Aswan, Kush and Nubia will attack the Deltan divisions on our right flank and scatter them into the eastern desert for the vultures to feast on."

"And Nekhebet's Camel Corps?"

Suti allowed Lieutenant Commander Nekhebet to speak.

"My Lord, tomorrow morning, I'll take my corps and two cohorts of the Nubian reserves across the Nile on pontoon barges. We'll move swiftly arcing out into the western desert…"

Nekhebet drew an imaginary arc on the map with his index finger.

"…and we will smite Hermopolis here, re-cross the Nile, and rush back south, attacking Memphis and the Delta on their rear. This should cause the enemy enough fear and confusion to allow Suti and Pawura to press forward their attacks."

Mentuhotep glanced at Bebi to ensure he was noting this down, then stared at the military map in contemplation. Suti raised his eyebrows.

"Is Pharaoh pleased?"

"General Suti, Pharaoh is exceedingly pleased. A great battle plan to assure us a crushing victory. More wine? A toast to our war-god Montu."

Chapter 17

Iset awoke and found herself lying on uncomfortable sacks of dried lentils below deck, having slept fitfully all night. She guessed the supply barge had docked and the bulk of the slaves and crew had disembarked, as it was very cold, dark and empty below deck and no noise resonated above her. Although, still quite weak, she felt this was her best chance to sneak off the barge.

Stumbling awkwardly off the lentil sacks, she moved cautiously towards the rear steps. The deck hatches had been left open to allow fresh air into the lower deck and she climbed slowly and silently up to the upper deck. Further down the long barge a couple of crewmen were sitting guarding the main gangplank, although, Iset could see they were dozing in the muggy afternoon sun. The rear gangplank had been set down on the quayside, obviously for fresh supplies to be brought aboard for the fleet's return to Thebes. Luckily for Iset, it remained empty and unguarded.

Still dressed in her boyish attire, Iset slipped down surreptitiously onto the dock and moved swiftly over to the safe shadows of the warehouses. Further down the quayside, she spied some Pharaonic guards standing gossiping idly in front of her father's Royal Barge. If Pharaoh caught her here, he would surely mete out the severest punishment, favoured princess or not. Her sketchy plan was to reach Suti's army to the north of Badari and find Achillas. Her plan, if she found him, was even sketchier. Iset motioned to slip up the alleyway between the warehouses into the city and then head northwards.

Before she moved, her eye caught a soldier talking with some guards at the bottom of the main gangplank of the Royal Barge. Her eyes could not believe what she saw. Achillas! The love of her life stood there as large as life.

*

Back at the war council, they conferred over the list of promotions and Suti had proffered up a large list of promotions and a smaller list of demotions, detentions and punishments for Mentuhotep's acceptance. Pharaoh was only interested in one particular promotion.

"Bebi will sign off all the changes on my behalf, except the one soldier I'm interested in. Is he here?"

Suti nodded.

"Yes, My Lord, although he thinks he's here as part of our guard escort."

"I'm glad he's unaware, as I wish to personally give this man his promotion and death sentence to his face."

Pawura looked puzzled.

"Death sentence, My Lord? I don't understand. This man's probably my best Greatest of Fifty officer and as loyal to Pharaoh as they come."

"That's where you are mistaken, Pawura. He has broken the code of his underclass and has attempted to steal the heart of my beautiful Princess Iset. For that indiscretion, he must be punished. But, I decree he should die honourably in battle. As a newly promoted 250 commander, I've commanded Suti that this soldier…"

Bebi pre-empted Pharaoh's hesitation.

"Achillas, Excellency."

"Ah, yes, Achillas. I've ordered this Achillas should be at the forefront of danger at every turn in the battle. His dead body will be returned to Thebes after our decisive victory and he'll be conferred a full military funeral."

Bebi half-joked.

"He could be buried in the royal necropolis at Abydos, My Lord."

Mentuhotep's eyes narrowed, as he scolded his Grand Vizier.

"That's a step too far for a commoner, Bebi!"

"A joke, sire."

Nekhebet had been listening intently. He knew of this Achillas and his reputation, but, Pawura knew him better, being one of his officers. However, Nekhebet saw a delicate and rare opportunity to further his own ambitions. His father was Prince of Kush, Pharaoh's nomarch for the princedom of Kush, and he spotted a chance to curry favour with Mentuhotep and place himself in line for an expeditious political marriage with Princess Iset.

"May I make a suggestion, My Lord?"

"Feel free, Nekhi, if it's to do with my plans for this Achillas."

"My idea's somewhat unusual, and certainly never been done on the battlefield before. On my advance tomorrow to the enemy city Hermopolis, I'm taking the 3rd and 4th Nubian cohorts along with my corps. Let's make Achillas the 250 commander of the 3rd cohort."

Pawura was astonished.

"Nekhi, there's never been a white 250 commander of a black cohort before! They'll tear him limb from limb or stab him in the back, especially, an officer they know little or nothing of a day before battle."

Mentuhotep was beside himself.

"An excellent plan, Nekhi. I love it."

Nekhebet continued.

"The 3rd cohort will be ordered into Hermopolis at the spearhead of the attack. The Hermopolitans hate the Nubians with a vengeance and will fight back with everything they've got. We'll sacrifice a few good men, with poor Achillas at the head of the column, but ultimately we'll take Hermopolis."

Pharaoh clapped with delight.

"Oh, bring this Achillas aboard to receive Pharaoh's honour. But, remember, my loyal officers, this stays between us."

Chapter 18

Achillas staggered off the gangplank of the Royal Barge like a bewildered drunkard. He could not believe what had just transpired a couple of minutes ago. Never in his wildest dreams did he imagine the golden was-sceptre of Pharaoh would touch his shoulder and confer him promotion to a 250 commander. He was puzzled about it being in command of the 3rd Nubian cohort, but he was far too loyal to his god-king to question the decision.

He crossed the quay towards the alleyway taking him into the Badari town centre. He needed a cool beer to celebrate before returning to camp to claim his 250 commander's uniform. It occurred to Achillas, celebration might not be the right word, as Mesehti's first prophecy struck him.

The promotion is not good news. It's designed to get you killed on the battlefront.

He shook his head, dismissing the prophecy as bunkum and entered the alleyway, looking for a tavern. About halfway down the alley he felt a hand tugging his arm and he moved to draw his sword.

"Achillas!"

He turned to face a small boy hiding in a doorway. The boy was dressed in a belted shendyt, the traditional short linen skirt, and a tight sailor's tunic.

"Who're you, lad? What's your business?"

The boy lifted the tunic to reveal breasts tightly wrapped in linen bandages.

"Achi, it's me."

He looked again and rubbed his eyes in disbelief.

"Iset! Is it really you, my love?"

They fell into each other's arms, smothering lips in smouldering kisses. Achillas held Iset at arms-length.

"Oh god, Iset. What have you done to your beautiful long black hair? And what's happened to your hands? They're in a terrible state."

"I ordered my slave to give me a boy's hairstyle. I've been on my father's supply barge as a slave on the oars since we left Thebes. My hair will grow fast and my sore hands will heal quickly, especially, after seeing you."

They urgently kissed again, holding each other as if they would never let go again. The two lovers slipped into a nearby eating house, acting like father and son. They ordered some leavened bread, stewed beans and two beers. Beer was the staple drink of all Egyptians regardless of age. Achillas spoke excitedly as they waited for their victuals.

"I've just left your father, Issi. He's promoted me to a 250 commander. A great honour."

"Is that not unusual, Achi? Pharaoh, my father, wouldn't normally attend...I don't mean to be rude...the promotion of a lower-ranked officer."

"I think it's because I've been selected for a very tough mission. He's put me in charge of the 3rd Nubian cohort to attack Hermopolis. But don't breathe a word of that to anyone."

A serving slave arrived with the food.

"Two plates o' bread'n hot beans'n two beers?"

They nodded and the food and drink was placed on their table. Iset looked concerned.

"I'm no military expert, but that sounds like a suicide mission. My father interrogated me about you, Achi, did he say anything?"

"He never mentioned your name. Just called me a hero of Thebes and said I was destined for greatness."

"Achi, my father has spies everywhere. He could easily have found all about you...about us."

They urgently clasped hands together. The eatery cook angrily shouted over.

"Oi! None o' that. We're not that kinda place."

Achillas laughed back.

"I'm a soldier of Thebes off to war tomorrow. I'm just

saying goodbye to my son."

"Sorry 'bout that, mate. Hail, Upper Mizraim."

The whole eatery stood up and began hailing victory for their army. An old crippled ex-soldier began singing, tears streaming down his wrinkled face.

"Come away the lads of Mizraim.

Let's march along to our Theban hymn..."

Chapter 19

Mentuhotep had proposed to General Suti, at the war council in Badari, that he sail his fleet further north and downstream on the Nile to be near the Mizri border. He also suggested visiting the battlefield to watch the spectacle of his impending victory. Suti would not hear of it. To have Pharaoh and his Royal barges put in harm's way was unfathomable. If Mentuhotep was harmed at all, it could have a devastating impact on the army's morale and the success of the campaign.

Suti suggested Mentuhotep return to the capital Thebes to prepare his subjects for their great triumph and the Pharaoh reluctantly agreed. The fleet of three barges began the slower return journey back upstream to the capital. Iset sneaked back aboard the supply barge, where she was brought to the attention of the Captain of the Whip. He had young boys of his own and accepted Iset's story she was a boy who had run off to join the army, but who was returning to Thebes after failing to enlist. Iset was put on light duties, serving food and water to the slaves on the oars.

When the desert darkness began rapidly descending, the fleet moored at the small port of Akhim for the night. The plan was to sail back to Abydos tomorrow, where the High Priests of the royal necropolis would conduct a religious ceremony to the gods for a decisive victory.

*

At the same time as the Royal fleet was mooring at the port of Akhim, Achillas, dressed in his new 250 commander's uniform, sat atop a sand dune, dejectedly saying his goodbyes to his comrade Mesehti. In the next few minutes he needed to report to his 3rd Nubian cohort and they would be crossing the Nile in the morning.

"It breaks my heart we won't be fighting side-by-side in the coming battle, Mesi. We've always looked after each other's backs in past fights."

Mesehti gave a friendly pat on Achillas's back.

"Hey, cheer up, Achi. You've just earned yourself a big promotion from Mentu the satisfied. What an honour and, if I say so, well deserved, my friend."

Achillas put his head in his hands.

"I don't know, Mesi. You predicted I'd get a promotion. But one, designed to get me killed."

"I didn't say you would actually be killed, though. Anyway, don't listen to Mesi. My old seer father made hundreds of prophecies. God knows how many he actually got right in his lifetime."

Tears streamed down the cheeks of Achillas.

"What if I don't see her again, Mesi?"

"You know, Achi. We always agreed, falling for a girl before going into battle was never a good idea. You've got it bad, mate. Who's it this time?"

Achillas hesitated, but what the hell, he would probably die in Hermopolis anyway.

"Princess Iset."

Mesehti visibly gulped.

"Oh god, Achi, no way. Pharaoh's youngest daughter! Does she even know you exist?"

Achillas choked back tears.

"She loves me with all her heart. Even stowed away to come and see me today in Badari. She was dressed as a boy and wanted to fight alongside me. I had to talk her out of it."

Mesehti shook his head.

"Achi, my friend, this is bad. There's no way Mentu's going to let you anywhere near his daughter. If he ever found out...if he hasn't already?"

"Makes your prophecy more believable, eh, Mesi? Look, I've to report to Lieutenant Nekhebet. I better get going."

The two soldiers embraced each other, possibly for the last time, and both stared wistfully south towards their beloved

Thebes. As they looked at the clear, inky star-filled sky, they both saw a large unidentifiable object travelling just above the southern horizon. They stared in awe and watched as the unknown object appeared to come down to land a good few kilometres to the south.

"What in the hell was that, Mesi?"

"No idea…a…a chariot of the gods?"

Surveying the southern horizon where the object had appeared from, a dreaded thought struck Mesehti.

"Look there in the sky, Achi."

Mesehti pointed low in the night sky and then traced a squiggle with his index figure. Achillas was none the wiser.

"You'll need to enlighten me. I don't know my stars, Mesi."

"Achi, that thing…that flying chariot thing…it's come from the direction of the Scorpius constellation. The scorpion!"

Chapter 20

The port of Akhim was a scene of general uproar and terror. Scared stevedores and warehousemen were scurrying away from the quayside towards the town. Even the Pharaonic guards were backing away from the Royal Barge in fear. Many of the sailors and oarsmen aboard the other two barges had fled towards the warehouses on the other side of the quay. Iset remained below deck. She was more fearful of being spotted by her father. She peeked out an oar-slit on the starboard side and saw a gigantic, silver oval-shaped spaceship, which had landed on the western desert side of the Nile, emerging from clouds of sand.

Back on the Royal Barge, Mentuhotep and Bebi, both as fearful as everyone else, were trying to put on a show of bravado in front of their subjects. They stood under the awning, partially ripped off its fixings by the force of the giant chariot-ship's landing, angrily waving their was-sceptres with ancient curses and incantations.

"Bebi, what the hell's that…that…thing over there?"

The vizier shook his head.

"I don't know, sire. I've heard of many stories from our ancients, handed down orally, of messengers of the gods who have visited us before."

"Are they here to punish Mentu, the god-king of Upper Mizraim? Are they angry about me going to war?"

Before Bebi could answer, a large door on the side of the craft opened with a great whooshing sound as the air-lock disengaged. Great beams of light shone out of the opening, lighting up the whole of the quayside. Great screams of terror arose all around, even as far away as the town centre of Akhim. Everyone fell to their knees and even Mentuhotep and Bebi prostrated themselves on deck.

A silvery metal gangplank extended automatically from

the craft's open door, down on to the flat sandbank, close to the Nile's edge. Two giant, shining metallic figures, the Bor-ak's AI robots, lumbered down the gangplank and stopped at the edge of the great river. Mentuhotep and Bebi were completely oblivious as to how laborious the effect of Earth's gravity had on the kinetic abilities of the machines.

Up in the mothership's geosynchronous orbit, the Commander observed the proceedings from the satellite camera zooming in on the port of Akhim. The on board computer was programmed to translate Bor-ak into various ancient blue traveller languages, including Mizri, the language of ancient Egypt. His spoken word was transmitted down to the lead AI and the giant machine boomed out in Mizri.

"Mentuhotep, ruler of Upper Mizraim, rise up and fear not. We have come to you in peace."

Pharaoh was sick to his stomach, but he felt he could not lose face before his people. He dragged himself and Bebi up onto the starboard rail, facing the silver flying machines, his whole body shaking with terror. He called nervously across the Nile.

"Who…who are you?"

"We have journeyed here from the red traveller, the one you call Horus the Red."

Bebi bowed reverently to the robots, speaking in a low whisper to Mentuhotep.

"Pharaoh, it's a chariot of the gods, from our great Lord Horus in the heavens. They must be here to honour you on the eve of battle, sire."

Mentuhotep called across the Nile again.

"What do you bring Pharaoh from my Lord God Horus?"

The Commander relayed his reply through the lead AI robot.

"The messengers of Horus request the presence of you and your vizier to meet us in our mothership in the sky."

Bebi looked at Mentuhotep in horror.

"There's no bloody way I'm going up in that thing, My Lord Mentu!"

Pharaoh looked back on the quayside, where bodies were edging forward with an air of expectancy. What was their god-king going to do? The robot boomed out again.

"Mentuhotep, there's nothing to fear. The machines will not harm you or Bebi. You have the true word of Horus."

After a moment's hesitation, Mentuhotep called across.

"Mentuhotep and Bebi will sail in your silver ship to meet the messengers of Horus."

Bebi stammered.

"I...I didn't agree to this."

Pharaoh considered the ramifications of leaving behind his Grand Vizier. If these damned messengers of Horus killed him, politically, this would place Bebi in a strong position. Bebi could even usurp his son, the young Mentuhotep, as the rightful heir to the White Crown of Upper Mizraim.

"Bebi, if I'm going on that bloody god-ship of Horus, then I command you to go with me."

"Yes, My Lord." Bebi was quaking with fear.

Chapter 21

The Commander relayed instructions for Mentuhotep and Bebi to sail across the Nile. Bebi arranged for a small flat-bed wooden ferry to be brought alongside the Royal Barge. The fearful ferryman and terrified son, his assistant, offered up their large barge poles to Mentuhotep and Bebi. The vizier scolded the two watermen.

"Don't be fools, men! Pharaoh and I couldn't possibly navigate the treacherous waters of the Nile on our own. You are commanded by your god-king to take us across to the shining silver chariot."

The ferryman shook his head.

"Not for all the bloomin' grain in yonder warehouse back there, I won't."

Mentuhotep removed a small pouch from his belt.

"What about ten of these?"

The two watermen stared at the pure gold sheep tokens, the pre-coinage barter system of the ancient Pharaohs. The ferryman nodded enthusiastically.

"I can buy me two grain stores with that there gold. We'll do it!"

"Pay the ferryman, Bebi."

It was low tide on the Nile and the river was not in flood, so the ferry crossing ended up easy money for the two watermen. Once they had landed Pharaoh and Bebi, the Commander relayed an order for the ferry to cross back to safety. The ferryman and his son had no intention of staying on the wrong side of the river.

The lead robot spoke again.

"Mentuhotep, Bebi, please board the spaceship and await further instructions."

Nervously, the two men edged slowly up the silver gangplank and into the brightly-lit cavernous interior of the ship. The two Royal Mizris were taken aback by the otherworldly technology, far beyond their comprehension. The two AI robots lumbered up behind them and, as the large door closed, the two Royal Egyptians realised there was no escaping their destiny. Once inside, they noticed two more metallic AI robots attending a bewildering array of flashing coloured lights. Towards the stern of the ship, Bebi was disturbed at what he spied and nudged Mentuhotep.

"Sire, we've made a huge mistake."

Laid before them looked for all intents and purposes like eight glass funerary sarcophagi, although much longer than wooden Mizri versions. Two of them whooshed open with a rush of air. Mentuhotep spun around and faced the lead robot.

"What is the meaning of this? Are we to be killed and interred here?"

The Commander tried his best to explain through the AI.

"Mentu, these capsules aren't going to kill you. They're designed to bring you safely into the heavens, where there's no air for a man to breathe. Inside you will see special garments to provide you with air and will protect you from great pressures exerted when the ship takes off. The robots will help you into these suits. It's also important you remain as calm as possible during the ship's journey. Being stressed is not helpful on your flight."

Bebi laughed half-heartedly.

"Stressed! Who's stressed?"

"We've come this far. We better do as the Horus gods command."

The robots assisted the two men into the spacesuits, made of luxuriously thick white material, neither had ever seen before. The robots then attached oval glass-like helmets to the spacesuits. The helmets and spacesuits were much larger than the men's bodies, but this did not alleviate their sense of claustrophobia. This was only heightened when the glass coffin-like lids closed on them. They lay side-by-side in the prone position and could no longer see each other. The Commander addressed them from the mothership.

"You can still talk to each other throughout the journey."

"Bebi, can you hear me?"

"Yes, sire, what is this magic?"

"I don't know, Bebi. But now I know what it was like for my father Intef, when we interred him all these years ago."

"Yes, Mentu, but at least he was actually dead!"

The spaceship started to roar as the pilot robot initiated the low fusion drive engines. Bebi yelped in terror.

"What manner of ship is this?"

Back on the quayside, bodies dropped to the ground in reverential fear of the gods. Iset, who had sneaked up on deck to watch her father embarking the strange craft, knelt in awe. Her father was indeed a god-king. She watched as the craft slowly rose into the sky, sand billowing all around, eventually seeing it reach an unimaginable height, before it shot off in a streak of light, heading towards the North Star. It would orbit around the magnetic north pole, continue on around the magnetic south pole, and then return to the equatorial region to dock with the Vor-maga I, in its fixed orbit over Africa.

Many of the soldiers of the opposing armies camping on both sides of the border, including Achillas and Mesehti, saw the streak of light zooming north through the heavens and most determined it was a prophetic sign from the gods. A good sign or a bad sign? That was anyone's guess.

Chapter 22

Surrounded by tall reed mace bulrushes, Achillas crouched in the sand dunes about a hundred metres from the South Portal of Hermopolis. Behind him, crouching and lying flat, was his cohort of the 3rd Nubians. Lieutenant Nekhebet, the Camel Corps, and the other cohorts remained about half a kilometre to the rear of Achillas. His orders were to storm the southern gate, smash into the city and engage with the enemy on a street by street basis. Nekhebet would follow up with the second wave in a mopping up exercise.

It had been a difficult morning for Achillas, after he had taken his cohort across to the desert of the western bank of the Nile. He introduced himself to over two hundred black soldiers, eyeing him suspiciously, as he was their first ever non-Nubian 250 commander and he spoke almost no Nubian. He had to relay all his orders in Mizri through one of his best Greatest of Fifty commanders, a huge powerfully-built Nubian named Kashta. Achillas had also realised the cohort had been ordered to take Hermopolis on a suicide mission, but his commands to his men tried to remain optimistic.

Achillas led the Nubians on an arcing route into the western desert to avoid early detection by the enemy. It was a twenty-five kilometre march in the sun's boiling heat to reach Hermopolis. He was exhausted by the time they reached their attack position in the bulrushes. The Nubians were renowned as great long distance runners and Achillas noticed most of them had hardly broken sweat. He surveyed the southern walls and saw very little activity on the ramparts. There was some smoke rising from inside the city near the portal. He turned to Kashta and spoke in a low voice.

"It's too quiet for my liking. That smoke might be the Hermies cooking breakfast, but they might also be boiling oil for us. Pass the word around, Kashta, tell the men to watch their heads when we reach the wall."

Kashta relayed the message and ordered it passed around. Achillas raised himself up on one knee, taking one last look at his objective.

"Right, Kashta, let the attack begin. I'll lead on the right flank with the first battering-ram unit, you take the left with the second battering-ram. The left and right wall-scaling units should be on our immediate rear, followed quickly by the remaining cohort. Keep it quiet as possible, unless we are spotted by the Hermies."

Achillas and Kashta drew their swords and waved them in a forward arc, moving out the units. The battering-rams were crude, thick palm tree trunks, just over two metres in length, with wooden spikes pinned to the trunks for the Nubians to carry. The wall-scaling ladders were of similar construction, although they were about three metres long, matching the height of the city walls of Hermopolis.

They snaked slowly and quietly at first, through about thirty metres of reed mace bulrushes, but sped into a trot across the low sand dunes when they broke cover. Everything remained silent on the ramparts, until the lead units were within fifty yards of the gates.

Suddenly, a hail of arrows, some burning, came arcing out from a line of archers on the ramparts. Alarm bells started clanging inside Hermopolis. Achillas screamed an order, quickly translated by Kashta.

"Raise your shields and charge!"

If a Nubian on the battering-rams was felled by an arrow, he was quickly replaced by a soldier running alongside in reserve. Although, the desert sand slowed the two ram units down somewhat, they reached the wooden gates of the South Portal fairly quickly and relatively intact.

Kashta screamed out an order from Achillas.

"Smash the gates open!"

The battering-rams started pounding on the Hermopolitan gates and Achillas and Kashta kept an eye on the ramparts overhead, peeking through their raised shields. The wall-scaling teams had also reached the city wall and began climbing as fast as they could. A few archers, who dared to peek over, took out the odd soldier scaling the ladders on the left and right flanks of the gate.

The remainder of the cohort stood back about thirty yards, using their shields to give Nubian archers protection, as they enfiladed the ramparts, providing defensive fire for Achillas and Kashta's units at the city gates and on the walls. Suddenly, Kashta, keeping his eyes on the ramparts over the gates, screamed out an order to the battering-ram units.

"Oil! Swing away from the gates, now!"

The two units reeled clockwise and anti-clockwise as the Hermopolitans poured a huge vat of burning oil down from the ramparts. It splashed and fizzed on the sand as the oil careered down. A few Nubians on the rams yelped as they received minor splash burns, but there were no serious injuries. Kashta ordered the units to swing back onto the gates and they pummelled the wooden doors again.

Meanwhile, a few of the Nubians had scaled the ladders either side of the gates and were sword-fighting the enemy on the inner ramparts. Everyone fighting hesitated as a great crack resounded across the town square. The header bar holding the gates shut snapped loudly and as the ram units pummelled the doors, they finally caved in, providing an open entry for Achillas and his men.

With a great war-cry, the remaining 3rd Nubian cohort charged forward towards the South Portal. Achillas and Kashta led their units inside the city, finding surprisingly less resistance than had been envisaged. The wall-scaling units had cleared the enemy fighters from the ramparts and they scurried down the stone steps to join the cohort now charging into the inner street. The few Hermopolitan soldiers that had guarded the gate were soon killed, a few captured and the others retreated down the narrow street towards the main square.

Nekhebet, astride his camel, ordered the remainder of his division forward at a slow trot. The grizzled Captain of the Camel Corps was puzzled.

"The 3rd have broken into the city, sir. Shouldn't we make a full-bloodied charge to give Achillas support?"

"All in good time, Captain. Let's give the 3rd time to show us what they're made of. Pawura tells me that Achillas is indestructible, so we'll give him a chance to prove that."

"But…?"

"We hold back meantime, Captain, that's an order!"

Chapter 23

The Earth orbit on board the AI robot-manned space-ship had literally been out of this world for Mentuhotep and Bebi. The metallic AI robots used electromagnets to keep themselves attached to the surface of the ship, but the Mizri leaders were allowed to experience the weightlessness of outer space, which they found both confusing and exhilarating.

"This must be what our ancestors experienced when they rode their death-chariots into the heavens, Bebi."

As the two floated around the cabin, the Commander issued an instruction via the lead robot.

"You must return to your spacesuits and capsules. We will complete docking manoeuvre imminently."

The two Mizris quickly complied assisted by the robots.

*

After the spaceship successfully docked with the huge Vor-maga I mothership, Mentuhotep and Bebi passed through the airlock. They were no longer weightless, although, they felt much lighter than on Earth. They were escorted by two Bor-ak guards who led them towards the bridge. The two Mizris were amazed at the sight of the Bor-ak. They appeared human-like, but they were giants in comparison, with bulbous craniums, narrow jaws and thin skeletal frames covered with sleek tight uniforms.

"What manner of men are these, Bebi?"

"I'm not sure, My Lord. The ancients say giants once roamed our lands."

The two men were guided on board the bridge by the two guards. They were astounded by the array of panels, lights, computers and monitors. Their operators swivelled around to catch a sight of their first humans. At the council table they were greeted by the Commander, the Chief Engineer and the Ship's Doctor. The Commander indicated Mentuhotep and Bebi should sit. The seats were designed for the giant Bor-aks and the two

Mizris felt somewhat self-conscious facing their large counterparts. Mentuhotep was brave enough to speak first.

"I'm Mentuhotep, Lord Pharaoh of Upper Mizraim. This is Bebi, my Grand Vizier. We know you're messengers of Horus the Red. What do you call yourself?"

The three Bor-ak officers had earpieces, which translated Mizri into Bor-ak. A translator device sat on the council table between the attendees, which transmitted back in Mizri.

"You call us the messengers of Horus. We call ourselves the Bor-ak and you're aboard our ship the Vor-maga I. Our names don't translate easily into Mizri, so I'm the Commander, this is my Chief Engineer and this is our Doctor."

Mentuhotep was astounded by all the technology, which was totally beyond him, but he did not question it.

"Why have you brought us up here to this great silver palace-ship in the heavens? Are we to die here, Commander?"

"No, Pharaoh. The Bor-ak are a peaceful race, unlike yourselves, our little sub-Bor-aks. We perceive you've the warlike instincts we suppressed many millennia past."

Neither Mentuhotep nor Bebi questioned what the Commander meant by 'little sub-Bor-aks'.

"Commander, I too am a man of peace, but my people were killed and raped. Our ancient sacred Necropolis of Abydos was desecrated by the army of Lower Mizraim. It is my duty to seek revenge, or else Pharaoh would lose great face before his subjects."

The Commander nodded.

"And the two great states of Mizraim collide in battle, even as we speak. See here."

The Commander pointed to one of the large monitors, which was focussing on North Africa. The Chief Engineer issued a command in Bor-ak to the Operator and satellite cameras began zooming in. At a certain point Bebi's face lit up in recognition.

"I don't know what this magic is, My Lord. But we are certainly flying above the Great Nile."

Pharaoh turned to the Commander.

"What is this trickery?"

"No trickery, Mentu. It is a camera attached to the ship, which can look at what is happening in Mizraim. A sort of eye in the sky."

Bebi tried to make sense of this god-like technology.

"The Eye of Horus!"

The camera continued to steadily zoom in, until it was focussed on the borderlands. To Mentuhotep and Bebi, it seemed they were looking down on two great nests of ants attacking each other. Bebi quickly made sense of it.

"Sire, it's the battle between our army and the Army of Memphis and the Delta. That must be Amarna to the north and Badari to the south. The armies are fighting each other in between."

From the height they viewed from, it was difficult to make out which side was winning. Mentuhotep turned to the Commander.

"Commander, use your God-given powers to intercede. Send your silver ship and the metallic giants to fight alongside the Army of Upper Mizraim. Provide Mentu his victory in battle and great riches will be bestowed on you."

"Mentu, there are no riches you own can help the Bor-ak. What we seek is a new red traveller out in the vast oceans of the universe, something you cannot bestow."

"I'll give you all the lands of Nubia and the Kush if you help me become ruler of all Mizraim."

"You don't understand, Mentu. Our Bor-ak race cannot survive on the blue traveller. Our bodies would be crushed on your lands."

Bebi interrupted.

"Sire, it looks like Suti and Pawura's forces haven't made any breakthrough yet."

Chapter 24

As the noise of battle raged ahead of them, Suti and Pawura conferred with their senior officers around a map table. Suti angrily thumped the crude wooden table.

"We aren't making fast enough inroads on the northern armies and soon it'll be sunset."

Pawura replied trying to console Suti.

"General, you're flank's trying hard to push Memphis around towards the Nile and my flank's trying to push the Delta forces into the eastern desert. Once we've carved open their mid-section, we'll flood through our reserve cohorts and cut them off. And so far, they're holding fast. But for now, their Rachotis and Rashid divisions are giving us hell in the centre."

"Where in the name of Osiris is Nekhebet? His orders were to take Hermopolis by surprise, cross the Nile and attack the enemy on their rear, allowing us to make the breakthrough."

Pawura shrugged his shoulders.

"There's been no word, sir. Maybe he's attacked the town of Amarna in a diversionary move?"

"I specifically ordered him to avoid Amarna, Pawura."

Suti pointed out at the raging battlefield.

"The enemy's not in Amarna. There's the fucking enemy army out there!"

*

Mesehti, who had replaced Achillas as one of Pawura's Greatest of Fifty, found himself in the thick of battle. His Theban company were struggling to force the Army of the Delta to wheel backwards towards the eastern desert. They found themselves steeped in bloody man-to-man fighting against companies of Rachotis of Alexandria and Rashid of Rosetta, who were putting up brutally fierce resistance. Mesehti smashed his sword left and right, as the sand below his feet stained black with the spilt blood of many men. Dead bodies and gruesomely severed limbs littered the battlefield.

Exhausted men were struggling to stand as they fought toe-to-toe, but they all realised the blackness of the desert night would soon descend and the horns blew on both sides, sounding the retreat for the day. Mesehti, struggled to lift his sword, as he waved his men back.

"Stop fighting, lads! Back to our own lines for tonight. Tomorrow's another battle."

As his company regrouped and trudged wearily back to camp, parties of stretcher-bearers passed them to retrieve the injured, before the hundreds of circling, black Egyptian vultures moved in to feast on the bodies strewn across the bloody field. Mesehti did a quick headcount and determined he needed to backfill eight lost men with young inexperienced reservists for tomorrow. The company would be weaker for it and he longed for Achillas back at his side.

*

Meanwhile, Achillas and his 3rd Nubians, were part of Nekhebet's military caravan making its way south, avoiding the city of Amarna as ordered by Suti. Nekhebet, riding his camel at the head of the train, was fuming on three counts.

Firstly, Achillas and the 3rd Nubians had single-handedly taken Hermopolis and the handsome young Theban had now become a great heroic figure, revered by his new cohort. Secondly, against the plan, Achillas had hardly a scratch on him and had survived the battle intact. The Hermopolitans on the western side of the Nile, had not envisaged the surprise attack on their city and it was poorly defended, with most fighting men marched south with the Army of Memphis. The 3rd Nubians quickly and easily overran the city.

Thirdly, when the alarm bells had rung in the city, many terrified refugees started fleeing in any available boats, rafts and ferries, heading for safety in Amarna across the Nile. This left the craft Nekhebet had planned to commandeer on the wrong side of the Nile and most boats the Hermopolitans left had been spiked and sunk in the harbour. It took much lost time to retrieve enough craft to ferry Nekhebet's division across to the eastern desert and get his army moving south again.

Nekhebet growled in angry frustration at the Captain of the Camel Corps as he looked at the quickening sunset.

"Keep the train moving for another half hour and then make camp for the night. I've a plan for the 3rd Nubians."

Nekhebet wheeled his camel around and rode back to find Achillas and his cohort. When he found them, all trudging wearily, he dismounted his camel and ordered Achillas to fall out.

"Great work at Hermopolis by you and your men, Achillas. I'll be recommending you for a commendation in my report on the battle."

Achillas harrumphed in disgust.

"We could've done with you and the rest of the division to back us up, sir."

Nekhebet lied.

"Our intelligence spies suggested the city was lightly defended. I didn't want the whole division rampaging through Hermopolis raping and pillaging. Thankfully, in the end, losses were minimal."

Achillas looked away in disgust and there was a sour pregnant pause, broken by Nekhebet.

"I've a problem, Achillas. We're way behind schedule and the plan was to attack the rear of the enemy divisions and allow Suti and Pawura to smash through and crush Memphis and the Delta."

"We'll arrive on the battlefield by noon tomorrow, sir, once we get a good night's kip at camp."

"That's too late, Achillas. I need a diversionary attack to harry the enemy first thing in the morning. I want you to lead the 3rd on a night march and be ready to strike at daylight."

Achillas was flabbergasted.

"Sir, my men are exhausted from the battle today…"

Nekhebet quickly interrupted.

"The 3rd are the best long-distance runners in my whole division and are well-trained in desert night marches. Once we camp, get them fed and watered and then I'm ordering you to lead the attack. I'll be there as quickly as I can muster the troops tomorrow."

"Yessir!"

Achillas stormed away in disgust.

Chapter 25

Iset was aware the crews and slaves were badly rattled by the appearance of the great silver sky-chariot. They were all becoming increasingly restless as time passed and showing concern that their Pharaoh had not returned from the heavens. Rumours were also filtering back from the battlefield that General Suti had not made any significant breakthrough. She overheard whispers of a possible mutiny from some aboard the supply barge and she felt compelled to act.

As dusk fell, she slipped quietly off the supply barge. Of the four Pharaonic guards on duty at the gangplanks of the Royal Barge, she recognised one of the longer-served guards. She strode over to the older guard and he immediately blocked the gangplank with his spear.

"Hey, boy, where d'you think you're going?"

"Lieutenant Raia, it's me, Princess Iset, daughter of Mentuhotep."

Raia studied the boy closely, then bowed in reverence, stammering a reply.

"Y-your Royal Highness. W-what are you doing here?"

"It's a long story, Raia, but I've no time to tell you it. I've uncovered rumblings of a possible mutiny amongst the crews."

"Mutiny?"

"Yes, and I'm going to need the help of the Pharaonic guards to keep order. I'll take temporary charge of the fleet until my father returns. Pass the word around but keep it quiet."

"Of course, Princess."

Iset stepped aboard the Royal Barge and she quickly found the Hebrew slave Ruth in the servants quarters. After a quick double-take, Ruth immediately recognised the sailor boy as Princess Iset. Iset ordered Ruth to take her to the female dressing cabin. Ruth looked out a crisp, fresh white royal dress for Iset, a kalasiris, with thick shoulder straps and copper cups for the breasts. Next, Ruth placed a brightly bejewelled neck-collar on Iset, and a perfumed wig of long tight curls and braids, interlaced with coloured beads. Finally, Ruth applied the heavy make-up befitting the style and beauty of a princess of Mizraim.

Ruth held Iset a mirror.

"There you are, My Lady, you're a princess once again."

"Thank you, Ruth."

Iset strode back out to the gangplank and saw Lieutenant Raia had ordered the full company of the Pharaonic guards onto the quayside.

"Lieutenant, have all the crews and slaves lined up on the quay, that I might address them."

Raia saluted and ordered guards to rouse everyone and within a few minutes a line of men stood before the tiny figure of Iset. She was nervous, as she had never addressed subjects before, but she had studied her father and began determinedly.

"For those who do not know me, I am Princess Iset, daughter of Mentuhotep..."

There was a distinct murmur along the line.

"...It has come to my attention many of you are fearful and distressed from the sight of the great silver ship, which has taken my father and his vizier Bebi into the heavens. I've heard talk of mutiny and desertion and I will not have it aboard my father's fleet."

The Captain of the Whip from the supply barge Iset had been on interjected.

"Your Royal Highness, I too have overheard these ugly whispers..."

He looked along the line of his own men.

"...I believe one of my boys has already deserted. But let me take the lash to these men and I assure you, I'll beat the mutiny out of them."

"Captain, there'll be no need for harsh discipline at this stage. And you can rest easy that the boy hasn't deserted, for I'm that boy."

The Captain of the Whip was horrified and he slumped prostrated in tears on the quay.

"Forgive me, Your Royal Highness, I…I didn't realise."

Iset walked over and gently helped the officer back onto his feet.

"Captain, you're a good man, a family man, and you showed me great kindness aboard your vessel. As for the rest of you, I want you all to allay your fears. I'm confident my father will be returned safely by these messengers of the gods. My father has great faith in General Suti and, I personally know we have some of the greatest warriors in all of Mizraim. They will bring us the victory we strive for. Meantime, I'll remain in charge of the fleet, which will dock here at Akhim until my father returns."

Lieutenant Raia barked out orders.

"Okay, men, you heard the Princess, so everyone back to their bunks and anyone steps out of line, they'll answer to me!"

As Iset stepped back on board the Royal Barge she mused on her words, *I, personally know we have some of the greatest warriors in all of Mizraim.* It concerned her that Thebe's greatest warrior and dearest love, Achillas, might not even be alive as the battle raged on.

Chapter 26

After a short recuperation period, the Commander called Mentuhotep and Bebi and his other officers back to the council table.

"Mentu, it is time to return you and Bebi back to the lands of Mizraim."

"Before we depart, Commander, can you show me on the Eye of Horus how the battle's going?"

"Of course."

The Commander pointed to the large monitor still zoomed on the borderlands.

"As you can see, Mentu, it is now night-time and there's no battle to see."

Bebi pointed to the Eye of Horus monitor.

"Are those stars?"

The Commander peered closely.

"No, Bebi, they're the faint twinkle of the opposing armies' campfires."

Mentuhotep pressed the Commander one last time.

"Join us, Commander. Help us secure a great victory and together we'll rule the known world."

"Mentuhotep, our mission's not to intervene in the lives of the sub-Bor-aks, merely to observe. I will warn you regarding two observations. Firstly, the world you know of is much larger than you could even dream of. Secondly, we Bor-ak learned over many millennia the art of war slowly leads to a path of ultimate destruction. The sub-Bor-aks should look towards the path of peace."

Mentuhotep beat his chest.

"Mentu *will* bring peace to all of Mizraim through the path of victory. But, if you haven't brought us into the heavens to fight alongside my army, why have you brought us here?"

"A good question, Pharaoh."

The Commander nodded to the Chief Engineer, who punched in the code, opening the top of the council table. The Commander lifted the reddish slab of carved rock and passed it to Mentuhotep. The two Mizris stared at the rock in wonderment.

"Mentu, this rock comes from our red traveller, the one you call Horus the Red. It contains an important message to all the sub-Bor-ak people and Bebi can take notes at this point."

Mentuhotep nodded for Bebi to get his papyri and pens ready, as the Commander continued.

"When our red traveller began to die many eons ago, we looked enviously at the blue traveller as our new home, but we found its strong force of gravity…"

Bebi stopped note-taking and interrupted.

"Gravity? What's gravity?"

"Hmm, good question, Bebi. Gravity's the force that pulls objects to stick on land. If you drop that rock, for instance, it will always fall to the earth. Does that make sense?"

Bebi nodded, as the Commander continued.

"When we came to research your blue traveller, we soon discovered this pulling force was much greater than our own planet, the red traveller's gravity. So much so, it would have been a crushing weight on our Bor-ak bodies. We then decided to send down our robotic machines to gather life forms on your planet and return them to Horus the Red for research. It took us a great period of time and we returned many different life forms back to the blue traveller. Some died out, some survived, many in less intelligent forms, but only one transplanted life form thrived with higher intelligence, technology and propensity for procreation. The sub-Bor-aks."

Bebi was struggling to maintain his notes with all the technical information. He pointed to himself and Mentuhotep.

"When you say sub-Bor-aks, do you mean us, mankind?"

"Yes, Bebi, mankind has been created in the image of the Bor-ak."

Mentuhotep looked at the giant hominid and raised his arms aloft.

"It's true, as stated by our ancestors, Bebi, we're created in the image of the gods. We *are* gods!"

The Commander laughed.

"We Bor-ak aren't really gods. In fact, like you, we also worshipped our own gods, who lived on our sacred mountain Vor-maga."

"Nevertheless, Commander, you are the messengers of the gods of Vor-maga, sent from Horus the Red, the one with the great eye in heaven. You have brought great knowledge to Pharaoh."

Bebi looked at the rock carvings.

"I can't make out what the carvings on the rock of Horus say."

The Commander indicated to Bebi to inscribe it on his papyri sheets.

"It is carved in Bor-ak and it states: *the last of the great beings of the red traveller sowed his seed among the beings of the blue traveller. Many seeds failed. One seed thrived and then there was the new being.*"

Bebi scribed furiously, as Mentuhotep looked puzzled.

"So, we're this new being, created by the beings of Horus?"

"Exactly, Mentu. This rock hewn of Horus is a record to mankind to retain for eternity. It should be carved onto your own rocks in various languages as a permanent record. Many eons into the future, we hope to return, as we've left some of our own seeds in the great southern land of ice."

Mentuhotep nodded.

"Bebi knows Egyptian, Nubian and Sumerian and he will arrange transcribed rocks to be passed down the generations. But, what's this great land of ice?"

"It's of no great consequence to you, Mentu. It's further away than you could imagine and it's too harsh for mankind to survive there. But it will safely store our Bor-ak seeds until our descendants can return, long after we all are dead."

"So Bebi and I can now return to Akhim?"

The Commander handed Mentuhotep a small silvery sphere.

"Take this sphere, Mentu. It is a beacon, sending my ship a signal. Should you need to contact me in the near future, smash the sphere to stop the signal and I'll send a robotic-manned ship for you."

Chapter 27

The eastern desert was icy cold and the moonless night was pitch black. It was difficult for Achillas, Kashta and the 3rd Nubians to trot across the featureless sand dunes. It was easy to get lost in the eastern desert, but, Kashta had brought forward a tall Nubian warrior, an experienced tracker. The Nubian flashed a sparkling white smile, which stood out in the darkness, and he pointed to the horizon. Kashta translated for the tracker.

"He says that's due south, Achi. We must keep heading for the tail of the scorpion in the sky."

Achillas mumbled indistinctly.

"Scorpius! Mesi predicted I'd be driven to the scorpion."

Kashta was puzzled.

"Mesi?"

"An old comrade of mine. Nothing to worry about, Kashta. Let's keep moving. If we make good time the men'll still get a couple of hour's kip before daybreak."

The cohort trotted double-time for another hour and it was now the middle of the night, if anything, even blacker and colder. Suddenly, the tracker who had been leading the night march came to a dead stop, bringing the cohort to a halt. Achillas whispered to Kashta.

"Ask him if he's spotted the enemy?"

Kashta conferred quietly with the tracker and they both began pointing into the sky.

"He says, out of the scorpion, Achi, look!"

Achillas saw the large silver chariot hovering in the sky away to the south. He could feel the dread ripple through his men. Was this chariot of the gods coming for him? Apparently not, as it quickly disappeared below the horizon and out of sight.

*

In the dead of night, the giant spaceship landed on the same spot as before, across the Nile from the Royal fleet tied up at Akhim. Again, terror rippled through the city and all those in the port. Princess Iset had to barter, with another ten gold sheep tokens, to get the ferryman and his son to take her across the Nile. She stood on the silted riverbank and as the craft's door opened, Iset's statuesque figure was bathed in the golden light beams. To everyone watching from the quayside, Iset exuded the air of the supreme epitome of a High Princess of Mizraim.

Mentuhotep, carrying the carved rock fragment, and Bebi, carrying his papyri scrolls, strode down the metal gang-plank, grateful to be back on dry land. The AI robots remained inside the ship. Iset ran to her father and hugged him.

"Iset? What are you doing here?"

"It's a long story, father. But we must take the ferry back across, to allow the flying chariot to rise into the heavens."

The ferryman was also eager to return to the safety of the other side. As he and his son punted their barge poles to steer the ferry towards the quayside, Mentuhotep raised the red rock above his head in acclamation.

"We have met with the messengers of Horus the Red up in the heavens above. They are giants of men and have given us this sacred message, that mankind has been created in their own true image. They must go soon on a great journey to seek a new abode in the stars, promising one day to return."

A rousing cheer rose from the quayside, resonating across the great river.

"Horus the Red has bestowed this sacred rock on the House of Upper Mizraim. Your Pharaoh will take this mighty message to the battlefield in the morning and use its magical powers to smite our enemies and gain our deserved victory!"

Another great cheer resounded, being cut short by the roar of the giant silver chariot of Horus rising smoothly into the sky, billowing great clouds of sand into the air and rudely cutting short Mentuhotep's speech as he choked on a mouthful of dust.

Chapter 28

Once the spaceship manned by the AI robots had safe-docked with the Vor-maga I, the Commander called his main bridge officers to the council table.

"We've safely delivered the message to the sub-Bor-aks and our mission here's complete. It's time for us to search for new worlds out in the galaxy and discover a new red traveller to settle on. Navigator, when is the optimum time for us to depart the blue traveller's orbit?"

The female Navigator surveyed the charts of the Vor system on her handheld monitor and computed her calculations.

"Sir, the best time for us to blast off is in twenty one of the blue traveller days, when Vor is shining on the land below us and the blue traveller moon is on the dark side. Then, we can achieve the optimal slingshot around our great Vor and thrust into deep space."

"Excellent. Set departure plans for twenty one days, Navigator. I'll use that time to continue observing the sub-Bor-aks. Although, I doubt whether our message of peace has entirely made its mark."

*

Achillas knelt on one knee and peered out into the desert, as the first rays of sunlight appeared in a stunning pinkish-blue sunrise. He was tired, and knew his men were exhausted, due to lack of sleep. They would need to use all their resources of adrenaline to give them strength for the coming battle. As the arc of the sun peered out of the distant Red Sea in the east, Achillas murmured a short prayer to Ra.

"Great Ra, if I've to fall today at the behest of Mentu, Suti and Nekhi, then let me die with honour and courage at the head of my men. Take care of my beautiful Iset and shine your golden rays on her always, that she should know I love her with all my heart."

Through the desert shimmer, he spotted two dark, ethereal figures running towards him. Kashta and the tracker returned from their recce mission and knelt beside Achillas, both gasping for air.

"Well, Kashta, what's your report?"

Kashta drew lines in the sand with his dagger.

"The Delta's positioned on our left flank and Memphis on the right, butted up against the Nile. They both have reserves to their rear, but there is a large unprotected gap between the two reserve lines, leaving their rear exposed in the centre."

"Great work, Kashta. We'll sneak up as close to the rear of their reserves without detection. As soon as we hear the horns and drumbeats signalling the advance of both armies, we will make our attack through the gap at full charge and pierce the enemy at his weakest point. We can only hope Suti and Pawura do their jobs too, or else..."

"What about Nekhebet, Achi?"

"He'll not be here for hours yet. Probably arrive in time to drag the vultures off our dead bodies."

*

Suti could not believe his eyes, seeing Mentuhotep in his war-chariot with his retinue arrive at the battle-camp. He was flabbergasted Pharaoh had also brought his daughter Iset to the fringes of the battlefield.

"My Lord, I thought we'd agreed you'd return to the safety of Thebes?"

"Change of plan, Suti. Much has happened in the last couple of days."

"But, Pharaoh, bringing your youngest daughter here, practically in sight of the enemy's army. It's no place for a girl."

Mentuhotep waved his hand dismissively at his overweight General.

"Fear not, Suti, we'll depart for Akhim as soon as you march into battle. And don't worry about my dear Issi. Her Royal Highness's bravery averted a possible mutiny, while Bebi and I were in the heavens."

"The heavens, My Lord?"

Bebi passed the red rock to Mentuhotep, as Suti looked baffled.

"Suti, I wish to address my troops, before they attack."

Suti made the arrangements to have his main front line paraded before Pharaoh and Princess Iset, both standing on the Royal war-chariot. Mentuhotep raised the rock above his head.

"Brave warriors of Upper Mizraim. I raise before you this sacred rock conferred to me by the messengers of our beloved god Horus the Red. I and my Grand Vizier Bebi were taken to their great mothership in the heavens in a fiery silver chariot..."

A distinct murmur rippled along the line.

"I saw that bloomin' chariot in the sky last night, while havin' a piss in the desert. Scared the livin' crap outta me, it did."

Pharaoh continued.

"This rock is a solemn covenant between Horus and the Pharaohs. We've been created in the image of the gods and they've bestowed their great benevolence upon us. We *are* their chosen people. This great rock confers supreme powers on your Pharaoh's army and will deliver us a decisive victory...in the name of...Horus!"

The soldiers began waving their swords, spears and bows in exultation and began chanting loudly.

"Horus! Horus! Horus!"

Bebi thought, privately, Pharaoh was using a great deal of political licence with the red rock, but, if it roused the army to victory, then it will have served its purpose. As Mentuhotep wheeled around to speed his war-chariot away, followed by his retinue, Iset implored him to allow her to stay here on the battle-field.

"No, Iset, we will return to Akhim and await news of our great victory."

*

On the other side of the battlefield the senior Lieutenant

Commander turned to face the General of the Army of Memphis, sitting astride their champing horses, surveying the field and hearing the enemy's roars.

"Suti's army sound up for it this morning, General."

"Then, we must ensure we hold the line this day. They'll try again to break the flanks between us and the Delta. Pass the word. The Rachotis must hold the centre at all costs."

Chapter 29

Suti and Pawura's front line simultaneously marched forward to the beat of the drums, their reserves moving parallel about 50 metres behind. The enemy remained on the borderline in their defensive positions, Memphis facing Suti and the Delta facing Pawura. With about 100 metres out from the enemy, Suti, riding behind the line, ordered the drumbeat to slow trot and the front picked up the pace.

At fifty metres out, Suti ordered the horns to blow the charge and Pawura did the same with his divisions. The soldiers of Upper Mizraim broke into full charge, using their shields as cover, and began chanting.

"Horus! Horus! Horus!"

Memphis and the Delta ordered their archers to fire at will and some of the Upper Mizris were caught in the enfilade, as a storm of arrows hailed down on them. As the swordsmen and spearmen charged forward, Suti and Pawura ordered their own archers to respond at will and many men on both sides started falling in the crossfire.

*

On board the Vor-maga I, the Commander and his bridge officers watched the unfolding battle for the white and blue crowns of Mizraim on the large monitor. The Chief Engineer was as appalled as the others watching the carnage taking place way below their orbit.

"Commander, do you want me to launch a robotic controlled ship to strafe the two armies and knock some sense of peace into them?"

"No, Chief, our mission's merely to observe the sub-Bor-aks. We must not get involved in their overall technological development. If they are like us in ancient times, in the future they'll master the supreme power to wipe out all life on the blue traveller. We won't be here to stop that happening."

*

The volleys of arrows in the blackened sky was the sign Achillas had waited for. He ordered Kashta to charge forward double-time and aim for the gap in the enemy's reserve lines. Racing in a pincer formation, the 3rd Nubians ran silently through the gap, shields up and spears pointing straight ahead. As they charged through, the mounted reserve officers were momentarily confused. Had reinforcements been ordered forward by the Memphis?

With twenty metres to attack the rear of the front line, Achillas screamed out the charge, and Kashta shouted in Nubian.

"Hit their archers first!"

The 3rd Nubians smashed the rear of the Rachotis like a herd of elephants crashing into a stone wall. General Suti quickly realised Nekhebet's forces had arrived in the nick of time and as the enemy's hail of arrows stuttered, he ordered the whole frontline to charge at full pelt. A great roar arose and Mentuhotep's army soon fell upon the enemy, with a great clash of swords, maces and spears. Men on both sides were embroiled in fierce hand-to-hand combat.

One of the officer's in the Memphis reserves realised what was happening.

"Those blacks aren't our men. They're Nubians!"

The officer was about to order reserves forward, when, suddenly, he wheeled his horse around at the sound of horns blowing. He was taken aback at the sight of a line of mounted camels charging on their rear. Nekhebet and his Camel Corps had charged ahead of the main division, which would take another two hours to reach the battlefield. Nekhebet roared an order as the corps galloped full steam towards the reserves.

"Don't fully attack the reserves, just harry them enough to disrupt and confuse them!"

The camels smashed through the two reserve lines, scattering men in all directions. The Camel Corps then wheeled around and headed back through the reserves, now in complete disarray. One or two camels were felled by enemy arrows, but in the main, Nekhebet's tactic was keeping the reserves out of the main battle.

Achillas, spattered in the blood of many dead foes, slashed his sword to and fro, and he felt that his Nubians were beginning to break the enemy flanks. All of a sudden, he could see the enemy was being turned back left and right and Suti and Pawura's forces were breaking through. As another man charged on him, he raised his sword to take him down, but was stopped in his tracks by a scream.

"Achi!"

Mesehti and his brave company had smashed through the enemy lines.

"Mesi, my god, is it really you?"

Before either could answer, the two officers found themselves fighting back to back, felling foes from all sides. More and more of Suti and Pawura's troops piled into the yawning gap. The plan to wheel Memphis back towards the Nile and the Delta into the eastern desert was working to perfection. The enemy were soon in complete disorder and hordes of frightened men were soon running from the battlefield in retreat.

Achillas and Mesehti, both bloody from battle, hugged each other as a crowd of Nubians and Thebans circled them cheering. The cry of victory filled the air and as the two warriors were raised onto their men's shoulders the chant arose across the battlefield.

"Horus! Horus! Horus!"

With the enemy in full retreat, Suti came riding up to the circle of troops celebrating victory.

"Ah, 250 Commander Achillas of the 3rd Nubians, if I'm not mistaken."

"Yes, General Suti, sir."

"I saw what your brave actions achieved today…and you *live* to tell the tale."

"The gods favoured me today, sir."

Mesehti quipped.

"Achi has more lives than an Egyptian cat, sir!"

The crowd burst into laughter.

"Well, men, carry on. I'm off to make sure Pawura and Nekhebet capture the Generals of Memphis and the Delta. Mentu the satisfied can then sue for peace and take all of Mizraim."

Suti rode forward along with his main army, chasing the enemy back northwards into Lower Mizraim.

Chapter 30

The walled city of Thebes was rammed to the rafters with thousands of cheering citizens as General Suti, astride his charger, paraded his victorious army through the main avenue towards the Royal Palace. Pawura and Nekhebet, rode behind him, waving imperiously at the crowd, accepting their adulation. The citizens heaped garlands of flowers and victory laurels on the necks of the proud soldiers.

Then followed, also on horseback, out of courtesy, the sullen captured Generals of Memphis and the Delta, then behind them on foot, the enemy's senior officers, who had been taken prisoner. The residue of the enemy Army of Lower Mizraim had been ordered by Suti to return to their towns, villages and fields, which they gladly accepted.

The remainder of the column entering Thebes was made up of cohorts and companies that had acted with distinction in battle, including Achillas, Kashta and the 3rd Nubians, Mesehti's Theban Company and Nekhebet's Camel Corps. The troops filed onto the main square and paraded in front of the palace for royal inspection.

The great painted doors opened to a fanfare of horns and Mentuhotep and his Royal retinue filed out onto the pillared balcony to a great roar, reverberating across the whole of Thebes. Achillas, standing to attention at the front of the parade, and Princess Iset, at her father's side, quickly spotted each other. A searing pang of love shot through their hearts.

Bebi passed the sacred carved rock of Horus the Red to his Pharaoh. Mentuhotep raised it ceremoniously above his head to a great cheer.

"Citizens of Thebes, this sacred rock, bestowed on your Pharaoh by the giants of Horus for all time, has brought us the great victory we prayed for. Suti's army gloriously conquered the enemy in battle and now Pharaoh will sue for a lasting peace with their defeated Generals. I fully intend to unite all of Mizraim into the greatest empire the world has ever known."

Another great cheer resounded, as Mentuhotep handed the rock back to Bebi.

"I will also be honouring our great heroes with batons, tipped with the silver Eye of Horus, in memory of the sacred god who delivered our victory."

Then with a cheer after each name, Bebi read aloud the heroic recipients, as slaves delivered the batons.

"Suti...Pawura...Nekhebet...Achillas...Mesehti...and the Nubian Kashta."

Word had spread to the city regarding Achillas's brave exploits at Hermopolis and the battle at the Nile. The citizens roared his name.

"Achillas! Achillas!"

Mentu was dissatisfied that Achillas remained a thorn in his side and Nekhebet was also secretly fuming. Mentuhotep raised his was-sceptre, modified with a golden spherical basket encapsulating the Bor-ak Commander's silvery beacon-sphere.

"Enough, citizens! I would like to make one final announcement. In recognition of outstanding bravery in the face of a possible mutiny, I wish to honour my daughter Princess Iset with an Honorary Lieutenant Commandership of the Theban division."

The crowd roared its appreciation and Iset coyly waved back.

"Finally, I now order my great citizens of Thebes to feast, drink and dance to the honour of our beloved gods Ra, Osiris, Montu and Horus. Any citizen found sober by tomorrow will be arrested and jailed!"

A great wave of appreciative laughter resounded across the main square.

As Pharaoh's retinue slowly filed back inside the palace, followed by the enemy delegation, under the watchful eye of the Pharaonic guard, Iset tugged at her father's sleeve.

"Father, do you expect me to attend the negotiations?"

Mentuhotep laughed.

"Not at all, my lovely Issi. It'll all be boring man-talk. Your command of the Thebans is purely ceremonial. You can go and pretty yourself up for tonight's celebration banquet."

Iset wheeled around too quickly and rushed for the exit, inadvertantly bumping into Nekhebet. He grabbed her shoulders to steady her.

"And where are you rushing off to, my pretty Princess?"

Iset stumbled for a lucid reply.

"I...I...just want to introduce myself to some of my new Theban division before they go carousing."

"Hmm, well, I'd like to speak with you later. My father, Prince of Kush, is one of the peace delegates. Following my great successes on the battlefield, he and I have a proposition for the Pharaoh. You might be interested in it."

As she quickly spun away from Nekhebet, she winced knowingly at the upcoming proposition.

Chapter 31

Outside on the palace balcony, Iset, her eyes squinting in the late afternoon sun, scanned the main square, still thronged with soldiers, priests, merchants, slaves and citizens. She searched in vain for any sign of Achillas. Taking a thin stick of charcoal and a scrap of papyrus from her eunuch slave, she scribbled some hieroglyphs.

"Take this note to the hero Achillas of the 3rd Nubians."

The eunuch bowed, took the rolled-up scrap and swiftly disappeared into the raucous crowd.

*

On the bridge of Vor-maga I, the Commander and his Chief Engineer had watched as the Thebans celebrated victory far below them. The Chief laughed.

"Looks like your fears for the warring sub-Bor-aks were unfounded, Commander. Mentuhotep seems to have quickly and resolutely brought peace upon the land."

"Mentu has certainly achieved his aim of uniting all of Mizraim, Nubia and Kush. He'll probably maintain that peace throughout his lifetime. But our observations over eons have shown us empire-building nations are beginning to emerge to the north of Mizraim, across the great middle sea, and also far to the east. Mentu has not eradicated all wars amongst the sub-Bor-aks."

*

Iset's slave searched high and low throughout the inns and taverns across Thebes, all crammed with jubilant warriors drinking merrily to victory. Eventually, he picked up a rumour Achillas was to be found in the Inn of the Glorious Falcon. The eunuch edged his way through the throng of drunken soldiers, who teased him mercilessly.

"Hey, pretty one! You want to be my ladyboy tonight?"

"My fat, ugly wife's back in Herakleopolis. Any chance

of a one-nighter?"

The eunuch turned on the drunks and huffed and puffed at them, his hand haughtily perched on his hip.

"I wouldn't give you lot the time of day. I'm looking for Achillas!"

The soldiers all burst into fits of laughter.

"Quite right, ladyboy, best go straight to the very top and satisfy our great hero of the hour."

One of them pointed to a corner of the bar, then shouted.

"Hey, Achi! There's a gorgeous lady looking for *you-who*."

The poor eunuch squeezed and squirmed across the crowded bar, suffering humiliating pinches, pokes and prods. He finally pushed his way through to a small round table covered in frothing pots of honey mead, where Achillas was celebrating with Mesehti, Kashta, the Nubian tracker, and a couple of other comrades.

"Achillas?"

Mesehti stood up unsteadily.

"I'm…Achillas!"

Quickly followed by Kashta.

"No, I'm…Achillas!"

The tracker moved to stand, but Achillas pushed him back onto his stool. Achillas was also pretty inebriated, with all the free drink passed his way.

"Don't listen to them, eunuch. I'm the real Achillas. But, safe to say…you're not my type."

The eunuch tutted huffily, as the drunken group burst into raucous laughter.

"You're not my type either, you big brute. I'm here to deliver a message from my mistress."

He passed the scrap of papyrus to Achillas, who had to cross his drunken eyes to focus.

Meet me. Nile Portal. Sundown.

Achillas knew it was from Iset.

He had never sobered up as quickly and nodded to the eunuch.

"Tell your mistress I'll be there."

The eunuch melted through the drunken, carousing warriors, who burst into song.

"Come away the lads of Mizraim.

Let's march along to our Theban hymn.

Let all our enemies retreat in fear.

When they see the gallant Mizris here."

Chapter 32

The last shimmering, orange arc of Ra disappeared below the distant horizon of the Sahara desert as Achillas arrived at the Nile Portal. Apart from one inebriated, snoring guard slumped against the gatehouse door, the gate was left open and unguarded. Everyone had gone off to celebrate the great victory. No-one else seemed to be around.

Achillas hissed a loud whisper.

"Iset?"

Out of the lengthening shadows, the beautiful young girl appeared.

"Achillas!"

The two lovers gladly fell into each other's arms, kissing urgently. Achillas held her at arm's length. Dressed in full royal garments, make-up and perfumed wig, Iset looked every bit a Royal High Princess.

"My god, Issi, you are the most beautiful thing I've ever laid eyes on."

Iset laughed.

"And you, my drunken friend, you stink of beer and stale sweat."

Achillas tugged at Iset's arm, teasing her, pointing through the open gate.

"Then let's bathe together in the sacred waters of the Nile."

"No, seriously Achi, what should we do about our dire situation?"

Achillas sobered somewhat.

"I don't know about you, Iset, but I want you as my wife. I love you."

"And I love you too. But my father...Pharaoh...he will never agree to us marrying."

Achillas held Iset's shoulders and fixed his gaze on her

beauty.

"Then, let's grab a boat out there on the dock and sail to Rachotis on the mouth of the Nile delta. We'll take a trade ship across the middle sea to the state of Athena. I'll become a paid mercenary for the Athenians."

Iset dropped her head.

"I...I don't know, Achi. What would become of me...?"

Before Achillas could answer, they were interrupted by two figures emerging from the gloomy alleyway. Nekhebet, full of drink, threw a small purse to the eunuch, who quickly scurried off into the darkening streets.

"Well, well, well. What have we here? You're a bit too cosy with a Royal Princess for my liking, Achillas."

Achillas put his arms protectively around Iset.

"Nekhebet? What in the name of Osiris are you doing here?"

"I'm here to claim my bride-to-be."

Iset screamed back at the sneering officer.

"I'll never be your bride!"

Nekhebet slowly drew his sword.

"Tomorrow, my father will be negotiating with Mentu, to bring our two great families together. One day I'll be the new Prince of Kush and you a High Princess of Mizraim. We're gods in our kingdoms. Achillas is a mere mortal and your father will never agree to your union with a commoner. So, Achi, let Iset go, get on a boat and get the hell out of Mizraim...or else!"

"Or else...what?"

Nekhebet pointed his sword at Achillas.

"Why didn't you die a hero's death in the war, Achi, like you were supposed to?"

Achillas sneered.

"Yeah, that's what Mentu, Suti and you'd planned for me, wasn't it? But, why did you and your Camel Corps come to my rescue? You could have held back and let the Nubians and I get slaughtered."

"First and foremost, I'm an officer and my duty was to bring honour and victory to Pharaoh. I prayed one of the Rachotis had run you through, but to no avail. So let's see if you've the nine lives of a sacred Egyptian cat."

Nekhebet waved his sword menacingly and Achillas steered Iset out of harm's way. Achillas had a short dagger, which he pulled from its sheath on his belt. The two warriors circled each other, just as the sleeping gatehouse guard began to stir.

"Oi! What's goin' on 'ere, then?"

Nekhebet spoke out of the side of his mouth.

"Stay out of this, guard. This is a private fight."

The guard, recognising both officers, mumbled a 'yes-sir'.

Nekhebet lunged forward with his sword, nicking Achillas on his left arm as he took avoiding action. Iset squealed at the trickle of blood on her lover's arm. Achillas moved to strike at his nemesis, but Nekhebet parried the dagger with his sword, a spark flashing from the striking metals. Another attacking lunge by Nekhebet wounded Achillas on his right forearm, the pain causing him to drop his dagger. Nekhebet encircled the disarmed Achillas and he began to pin him back onto the gatehouse wall.

"Prepare to die, Achillas. To the winner, the spoils of victory."

Nekhebet lunged in for the kill, but Achillas reacted quick-wittedly, grabbing his enemy's sword arm and the weapon clanged noisily against the wall. The two angry soldiers wrestled each other, trying to gain control of the sword.

Suddenly, Nekhebet stared wild-eyed at Achillas. He felt as if he had been punched in the back below his ribcage and he staggered backwards, turning slowly to face Iset. Feeling his back, he discovered the dagger deeply embedded and he knew it had punctured his heart. As the life drained from him, Nekhebet collapsed onto his knees and croaked.

"By Osiris, you've killed me, Iset."

Chapter 33

Mentuhotep could hardly believe he and Bebi were back on board the low gravity mothership, Vor-maga I. Pharaoh had smashed the metallic sphere, signalling he needed help from the Bor-ak Commander. Once again, they sat at the bridge council table, facing the giant Commander and his Chief Engineer.

"Well, Mentu, I didn't expect to see you again. We leave the orbit of your blue traveller in three days on our great journey across space. But, you've called for my help?"

Mentuhotep lowered his head.

"Commander, I should be celebrating my great victory at the Nile and the signing of the great Treaty of Mizraim, brought about by the rock of Horus, but instead, my heart's broken."

The Commander shook his head.

"Pharaoh, the rock has no real mystical powers, it's a message from the Bor-ak for mankind. But, if it inadvertently has brought about peace, then maybe that's a kind of magic. Why's your heart broken?"

Mentuhotep was too choked to speak and he waved for Bebi to continue.

"My Lord is distraught over his beloved daughter, the Princess Iset. It appears she killed a Lieutenant Commander Nekhebet to save her soldier lover Achillas, as alleged by a gate-house guard who was a witness to the killing. Achillas and Iset escaped on a boat and are sailing for the Nile Delta and middle seas beyond."

The Commander looked on Pharaoh with pity in his eyes.

"Do you want them back, Mentu?"

Bebi continued as hot tears ran down Pharaoh's cheeks.

"If Achillas and Iset are brought back to Thebes, then Pharaoh would be bound by Mizri law to try and execute them for murder."

"So, you want them to escape?"

Mentuhotep cried out in anguish.

"I don't want to lose my daughter. But if the war hero Achillas and Princess Iset sail from Mizraim, at least I can let her live."

The Commander was puzzled.

"Then surely you should let them go?"

"Iset was to be betrothed to Nekhebet. As soon as his father, the Prince of Kush, heard of his son's death, he sailed off with his guards on board his barge, vowing to avenge his son. He's sure to catch them, but if he touches a mere hair on my daughter's head, then by the rock of Horus, Kush will be at war with Mizraim."

As the Commander mulled the problem over, the Chief filled the pregnant pause.

"Commander, you often remind me our mission is merely to observe the sub-Bor-ak…"

The Commander raised his hand.

"Mentu, the Chief has a valid point, so what is it you're asking of me?"

Mentuhotep pointed to the monitor.

"Use the mystical Eye of Horus. Find my daughter and her lover before the Prince of Kush does and rescue them. Take them away with you up to the heavens."

*

The dawn would soon break in the eastern desert. Achillas worked hard to steer the tiller of the little boat in the darkness, whilst Iset expertly tacked the sail. Iset had used the years spent aboard the Royal Barge on the Nile to learn the art of sailing from her father's naval officers. They had hardly spoke to each other throughout the cold desert night, after fleeing from the port of Thebes, both wallowing in the guilt of Nekhebet's death. Although, in their eyes, it was self-defence, they knew staying would mean a death sentence for both of them.

Looking back towards the Upper Nile, Achillas yearned

for his beloved Thebes, the city of his birth, but he believed they would never see it again. He knew Iset would be feeling the same emotions, but he could not find the right words to console her. Suddenly, looking back, he made out lights bobbing in the gloom upriver. It could only mean one thing.

"Issi! There's a barge bearing down on us. Fast, by the look of it."

"Then we're doomed, Achi."

Achillas did not want to agree with Iset and he stared back at the approaching lights. He struggled to foster a plan that would save them and stared up into the heavens in prayer. His eye caught the sight of that prophetic constellation once again, hanging just above the southern horizon. Scorpius! Then, once again, out of the sign of the scorpion, emerged a much larger light, getting bigger and tracking in low over the Nile. It was the giant silver chariot of the gods.

The spaceship's searchlight caught the Prince of Kush's barge and the little escaping skiff in its powerful beam and it revealed that there was only about two kilometres between them. Kush would exact his revenge in the next few minutes. However, the downdraft from the landing spaceship rocked both vessels violently. The Prince of Kush, who was standing on the bow-rail of his wildly rocking barge was tipped overboard. His Captain ordered the slaves to stop rowing and some guards jumped in to rescue their floundering master.

The boat carrying the two star-crossed lovers canted over steeply. It began shipping water and quickly sank into the muddy waters of the Nile. Both Achillas and Iset, carried by the strong currents downstream, struggled to swim towards the western bank. Iset was coughing in river water and Achillas was struggling to keep her afloat. By a stroke of great fortune, they were both thrown up onto a reedy sandbar jutting out into the great river.

They both lay coughing up the muddy water. Then, all of a sudden, they were enveloped in a sand storm, as the silver chariot in the sky landed about a hundred metres away in the western desert. The door slid open with a whoosh and the metal gangplank was automatically lowered. Iset could not believe her eyes. Her father Mentuhotep and Bebi exited the silver ship and urgently beckoned them over.

"My god, Achi, we really are doomed. My father has the gods of Horus on his side."

Chapter 34

Transferring from the Bor-ak silver sky chariot to the gigantic mothership, Achillas and Princess Iset were astonished by the mind-boggling scale, size and technology of the Vor-maga I. The tiny princess felt miniscule compared to the giant Bor-ak crew members, as the four Mizris made their way to the bridge. Crowding around the council table, the Commander was deeply struck by Iset's beauty. Knowing the sub-Bor-aks were a mutated species of his own race, even he was surprised they had been able to create such a beautiful female. It was no wonder so many sub-Bor-ak men had fought over and even died for the love of this princess.

The Commander spoke first.

"Mentu, you have asked me to rescue your daughter Iset and her lover Achillas from the vengeance of the Prince of Kush. What would you like to say to her?"

Mentuhotep spoke a little sheepishly.

"My beautiful Issi. It's difficult for your Pharaoh…your father…to find the right words to say at a time like this. My logic tells me Bebi and I must return you and Achillas to Thebes and have you tried and executed for the murder of Nekhebet…"

Iset cried in anguish.

"I swear it was self-defence, father. Nekhebet attacked Achillas unprovoked."

Achillas spoke up.

"I killed a senior officer in a duel over Iset. The princess, your daughter, had nothing to do with it. Take me and try me if you wish, Pharaoh, but let Iset go free."

Mentuhotep raised his was-sceptre for silence.

"Quiet, both of you! There was a witness, the gatehouse guard, who testified to what he saw. But, putting that to one side, I've no wish to return my beautiful Princess Iset or you, Achillas, the great hero of the Nubian cohort, and have you both beheaded in front of the baying mob on my palace square. I can see you both have an unbreakable bond of love for each other...but... what to do with you?"

Achillas spoke again.

"Pharaoh, may I speak?"

Mentuhotep nodded his agreement.

"Pharaoh, these gods from Horus have the ability to take us away from Mizraim. Iset and I were fleeing to Athena. They could fly us in their silver chariot and I'd become a professional mercenary...or even an ambassador of Mizraim...in Athena."

The Commander agreed.

"I'd happily take Iset and Achillas to this Athena."

Pharaoh shook his head.

"It wouldn't work. The Prince of Kush has feelers all across our known world. He'd eventually find them and have them assassinated. My proposal is for Iset and Achillas to fly off with you Commander, on board the Vor-Maga I and seek out new worlds, far beyond the tentacles of Kush."

The Commander and the Chief Engineer looked at each other and shook their heads.

"That's impossible, Mentu. When the Vor-maga I leaves the Vor system, the system you call Ra, we have to go into a deep cryogenic sleep for many years..."

Bebi, trying fruitlessly to take notes, was bamboozled.

"A what kind of sleep?"

The giant Commander stood up, towering over the four Mizris.

"Come! I'll show you."

The Commander, his Chief, both wearing translator mics, and the four Mizris filed into an elevator, taking them from the bridge, down three levels to the cryogenic hold. To the four Mizris, astounded at the sight, it looked like a huge gallery full of large crystal sarcophagi, similar in shape to the capsules, which brought them on the robot-controlled ship.

The Chief Engineer ushered them over to the first two

capsules on the left-hand side of the gallery. Two Bor-ak figures, a male and female, wrapped in fine white transparent shrouds, lay inside the capsules. Bebi pointed them out to Mentuhotep.

"Look, My Lord. These two messengers of Horus have passed over to the other side and are making their final journey in their sarcophagi to sit in heaven with the gods."

The Chief put his large hand on Bebi's shoulder.

"You really think they are dead, Bebi? No, they are cryogenically frozen…they are being kept in a deep sleep. These two are part of our research project and they are beta-testing the cryogenic capsules to ensure they work properly. They will be re-awakened before we depart the Vor system to ascertain whether the system has been working perfectly. Once we pass through the great asteroid belt and into deep space, all aboard, including the Commander and myself, will go into a deep-freeze sleep until the Vor-maga I can seek out a new red traveller for us to colonize."

Mentuhotep turned to the Commander.

"I implore you, Commander, take Princess Iset and 250 Commander Achillas with you to this new red traveller?"

Iset cried out.

"No way, father! I'm not going in any glass coffin to god know's where in the heavens."

The Commander raised his hand.

"I'm sorry, Mentu. But Iset's right. There's no way I can take your daughter and Achillas into deep space. I've only enough capsules for all of my own crew, and anyhow, they've been developed to keep our Bor-ak bodies alive. We've no idea if sub-Bor-ak bodies would survive such a trip."

The Chief Engineer concurred.

"Sir, I agree the risks are far too great. Anyhow, taking just Iset and Achillas would also be totally unfeasible. Taking just two beings from a single species would not be enough to help procreate a whole race on a new world."

Mentuhotep raised his arms in exasperation.

"What can I do then, Commander? Take them back to Mizraim and execute them. Or let Kush have them assassinated in Athena, with the risk of a new war."

"Let's return to the bridge."

Chapter 35

Seated around the council table, the Commander led the discussion for a resolution to Achillas and Iset's plight. He fully reiterated it was impossible to take the two star-crossed lover's on the Vor-maga I's research mission to find a new red traveller. The Commander recognised returning them to Thebes or across the middle sea to Athena, presented a dangerous outcome, unlikely to end well. However, he insisted that Achillas and Iset must be returned to the blue traveller. Mentuhotep was unconvinced.

"But, Commander, if you can't take them to your new world in the heavens, how can they possibly survive in the old world on land?"

The Commander paused a moment in thought.

"Mentu, you've just hit on a solution."

"Me? What solution?"

"The blue traveller *has* a new world. One that your old world has never seen or knew existed. We could take Achillas and Iset there to start a new life together."

Achillas interrupted.

"Now, wait a minute. Everyone's talking about Iset and me as if we'd nothing to say about it. I mean to say, would we be the only man and woman in this new world?"

"No Achi, this new land has a race of people, who aren't as technologically civilised as the Mizris, but they're as intelligent and industrious. They call themselves the Norte Chico people. You and Iset would be able to bring them great advances in civic architecture, agriculture, irrigation and much more."

Iset was dubious.

"Achi, is that something you and I could do?"

"Certainly not on our own, Iset. We'd need a team of experts along with us."

Mentuhotep was becoming quite optimistic about a solution to his thorny problem.

"Achillas, if you choose some comrades you can trust, I can supply a few experts in architecture and agriculture. Bebi can throw in a couple of viziers and priests. You and Iset would be given overall command of the expedition to this new world. But…Commander, how can you be so sure they'd be beyond the tentacles of the avenging Kush?"

"Let me demonstrate."

The Commander instructed the female Navigator to take the Vor-maga I out of its geosynchronous orbit and into a geocentric orbit travelling east to west. Bebi asked, for his papyri notes, how high above the blue traveller they orbited and the Commander tried to explain it in layman terms.

"The Mizri unit of measurement is the royal cubit, Bebi, is that correct?"

Bebi extended his forearm, which was the standard basis of measurement in Mizraim, and he nodded in agreement.

"Then, we're currently rising to an orbit of about eight hundred thousand cubits above the blue traveller."

Bebi sneered in disbelief.

"Bah, what nonsense. There's no such number."

"Trust me, Bebi, there's no limit to numbers. They go on and on into infinity, which the sub-Bor-aks will one day discover. In the same way, the universe has no end to it and its size is even beyond our Bor-ak imaginations."

Bebi just scribbled the hieroglyph for 'very high'.

The Navigator confirmed the mothership was in its geocentric orbit heading west and she turned on the large monitor, the one Mentuhotep called the Eye of Horus. The Commander pointed to the screen and described as best he could, to the wide-eyed Mizris, what they were looking down on. Bebi tried his best to sketch a crude map of what he saw below.

"You'll see we're travelling west away from the western desert of Mizraim and across the great expanse of the Saharan desert. To the north you can see the great middle sea, where you conduct your seafaring trade. On the other side is Athena, Sparta and other parts of Magna Graecia."

Mentuhotep was dumb-founded.

"But…it's all so small."

"Believe me, Mentu, your blue traveller and our Horus the Red are mere specks of dust in the vast ocean of space."

They all watched in silence for a few minutes as the mothership continued its orbit.

"We've now reached the end of your old world. Below you can see the western end of the middle sea and the Keftiu Anedjti. The Athenians call them the Erákleiai Stílai or the Pillars of Hercules. Here, the middle sea flows out into the vastness of a great western sea."

Bebi was finding it difficult to comprehend.

"But it takes a Phoenician trireme over a month to sail across the middle sea from Rachotis on the Delta to the Keftiu. My guess is we've covered that distance in less than half an hour. How can this be?"

"Bebi, you've already found it hard to understand the number of royal cubits high we are. You wouldn't believe the number of cubits required to describe how fast we're flying."

They all continued watching in silence, as the mothership continued its orbit across the vast blue ocean of the great western sea. Achillas broke the silence.

"All this blue below us, is it all water?"

"Most of your planet is covered in water and that's why the Bor-ak called it the blue traveller. Long ago, our red traveller had great seas and vast oceans and teemed with all manner of life forms, but no more. That's why we looked enviously towards this blue watery world, but in the end it couldn't support the Bor-ak."

The deep blue sea began to give way to the outline of another land and the Commander pointed to the monitor.

"Ah, we have reached the eastern side of the new world I spoke of. The Norte Chico people are on the western side of this vast land, far beyond the great steaming rain forests and across the high western snow-capped mountains."

Mentuhotep was stunned by the abounding verdancy of this new land.

"From up here, it's like the head of a gigantic green lion looking back towards Mizraim."

Bebi, again trying to sketch a map, also commented on the shape of the land to the Commander.

"Pharaoh's correct. It's indeed like a huge lion's head, Commander. A very good omen in our Mizri culture. The lion is a lower god-creature, representing protection and the defeat of chaos. This great land of the lion will be the protective barrier for Iset and Achillas. Kush will never find them."

Once across the western mountains, the Commander ordered the Navigator to lower the mothership back into a geo-synchronous orbit. He explained, they were now high above the lands of the Norte Chico people and he zoomed down to outline the rudimentary cities and villages carved into the foothills of the jagged mountainous barrier, looking out over a vast eastern sea.

"There we have it, Mentu, a new world for Achillas and Iset, far beyond the reach of the Prince of Kush and even you, Pharaoh. Well, you two lovers…are you prepared to start a new life down there?"

Achillas and Iset conferred quietly with each other. Iset spoke.

"Achi and I are prepared to start anew as husband and wife, if we can have the comrades and experts, promised by my father, for this expedition."

The Commander felt they had reached a satisfactory solution, but he was puzzled by one point.

"That's good…but what's a husband and wife?"

Mentuhotep laughed.

"250 Commander Achillas and Princess Iset want to have a wedding to confer their union. Mentu is satisfied. I give it my honourable blessing and Bebi will arrange the ceremony."

Chapter 36

The four Mizris were brought back down to Thebes, the robotic craft landing beside Suti's army camp close to the city. It was agreed Achillas and Iset would remain on board for their own protection, which neither was particularly happy about. They would be guarded inside the craft by the AI robots and Mentuhotep ordered Suti to throw a ring of armour around the chariot of Horus. Bebi made arrangements for food and drink to be supplied to the ship for Achillas and Iset.

Mentuhotep and Bebi returned to the Royal Palace to make plans for the new world expedition. Coincidentally, the Prince of Kush's barge arrived back in the port of Thebes on the same day and he demanded an immediate audience with the Pharaoh. Kush was fuming.

"My Lord Mentu, have you returned with the assassins of my beloved son Nekhebet?"

Mentuhotep shook his head.

"I'm afraid not, Kush. I tried for hours to negotiate with the giants of Horus to have Achillas and Princess Iset released into my custody. I'd have brought them back to be tried for murder, but their Commander refused to release them from the heavens."

Kush banged his was-sceptre on the marble floor.

"Then, we must attack these giants of Horus and wrest back the criminals and avenge my son's death!"

"Hah, Kush, and I take it you can fight giants and have winged chariots that can fly into the heavens...how many royal cubits was it Bebi?"

Bebi consulted his papyri notes.

"Um, a 'very high' number, My Lord. Too many for any Mizri to even comprehend."

Kush was far from satisfied.

"So, what do the Horus lot intend to do with Achillas and Iset?"

Mentuhotep considered his answer.

"I'm sure I've no idea. Bebi, do you know anything?"

"Well, My Lord, I overheard the leader of the Horus say he'd agreed to send the two young lovers in one of their flying chariots to Athena."

Kush thumped his fist in his open hand.

"I guessed that's where they were escaping to. Well, I'll hunt them to the ends of the earth and wreak my vengeance. Do I have your blessing, Pharaoh?"

Mentuhotep placed his was-sceptre on the prince's shoulder.

"If you find them, you have Pharaoh's blessing to try them and execute them and throw their miserable bodies into the Aegean Sea. And please send my humble greetings to the King of Athena and inform him Mentuhotep has united all of the great lands of Mizraim."

The Prince of Kush bowed and swept out of the palace.

"Well, Bebi, d'you think he bought that steaming pile of camel dung?"

"I doubt it, My Lord. He could still cause trouble, if he keeps his eyes and ears open. You know what the palace is like… like a leaking sieve."

Chapter 37

Later that afternoon, Mentuhotep and Bebi arranged a series of preparatory meetings in relation to the impending great expedition. The first one was with his wife, the one Pharaoh could never quite remember her name, Iset's mother; his older daughter Princess Meketaten, the plain one, and the extremely attractive Hebrew slave Ruth. The three women prostrated themselves on the floor before Pharaoh.

"My dearest wife, mother of Iset, I bring news your daughter's safe in the hands of the giants of Horus."

"Oh, praise Ra. And you'll pardon her when she returns to Thebes, My Lord?"

"Iset can never return to Mizraim. Pharaoh would have to mete out his royal justice or lose face with Kush."

Iset's mother was crestfallen.

"What's to become of her?"

"Well now, this is where you three ladies come in. I have agreed that Achillas and Iset are to be wed…"

"Iset married, My Lord, to a commoner?"

Mentuhotep angrily banged down his was-sceptre.

"Silence, woman, let Pharaoh speak! I've consented to them being married on board the flying chariot. You three will attend the wedding and then you will join Achillas and Iset on a great quest to a new world, beyond the clutches of Kush."

The three women began weeping, fearful at the thought of having to go on the alien craft and being transported to a new unknown world. Mentuhotep tried to placate them.

"Oh, please do stop crying. Wife, I formally annul our marriage, and set you free to take a new husband in this new world. You'll also be with your beloved daughter Iset. Meketaten, you'll be Iset's bridesmaid, and by going on this expedition, I free you from marriage with that old sop Suti. But, leave him to me, I'll find him another princess to wed. And, as for you, my slave…"

Mentuhotep looked at Bebi.

"Ruth, sire."

"…Ah, yes, Ruth, you will depart on this quest as a free woman, to do as you will and marry whomsoever you find love with in the new world."

*

The next meeting was briefer, with two viziers and two eunuch priests in attendance, hand-picked by Bebi. Although they were startled at the prospect of flying off on the winged chariot to some new world, they knew they had no choice but to follow their Pharaoh's command.

*

The final meeting was with the two Greatest of Fifty Commanders Mesehti and Kashta, the tall Nubian tracker and the Captain of the Whip of the royal supply barge. Mentuhotep explained about the impending wedding and Mesehti would be best man to Achillas, now promoted to General Achillas, and also that the five military men would lead the expedition to the new world. Mesehti begged to address Pharaoh, which was granted.

"My Lord, in my dreams, I've seen this new world on the far side of a great sea. I have foreseen that Achillas and Iset will become great leaders amongst the people of this new world and they will achieve great things. I for one, will be honoured to serve them."

Mentuhotep was taken aback, almost as if Mesehti had seen through the Eye of Horus on the mothership, as he and Bebi had.

"The giants of Horus also showed us this new world far beyond a great western sea. Thus, your prophecy bodes great hope for Achillas and Iset's future. And, with you four by their side, managing their new army and navy, a New Mizraim will rise far from the vengeance of Kush."

The Captain of the Whip stated he would be honoured to serve Iset, however, he had a wife and four sons in Thebes. Mentuhotep offered a concession to the sailor.

"The expedition leaves tomorrow after the wedding. I've arranged with the leader of Horus for a second flying chariot to arrive in the morning, as two ships are required to take everyone to the mothership and thence to the new world. You may take your wife along with you, Captain, but your four sons must remain to serve in Pharaoh's navy."

Chapter 38

A dazzling red sunrise rose out of the Red Sea on the morning of the wedding. A pre-wedding breakfast banquet was arranged by Mentuhotep in the elaborate State Room of the Royal palace for the departing guests, who would attend the wedding of Achillas and Iset on board the Vor-maga I later that day. Bebi, sitting next to Mentuhotep, could never in his wildest dreams have imagined such an eclectic gathering of royalty, clerics and low commoners dining, talking and laughing together. Around the long, low-slung marble table, Bebi and Mentuhotep sat beside Iset's mother, Princess Meketaten, the Hebrew named Ruth, now a free woman, two viziers, two eunuch priests, Mesehti, Kashta, the Nubian tracker, the Captain of the Whip and his attractive wife. Slaves were busily coming and going, ensuring that everyone was amply served with great platters of food and plenty of Egyptian mead and wine. Mentuhotep was in an ebullient mood and full of jest.

"Well, ex-wife of mine, at least my father Intef ensured you and I got to enjoy our pre-wedding banquet."

Iset's mother smiled coyly, still in hushed awe of her Pharaoh, although technically, he was no longer her husband.

"But don't worry, my dear, I've sent plenty baskets of celebratory breakfast over to the winged chariot. I just hope that General Achillas stays sober enough to enjoy his nuptials tonight. I expect him to provide us with many grandchildren in this new world."

Mesehti laughed and raised his cup of sweet, frothy beer.

"Leave it to me, My Lord. I'll be drinking out of Achi's cups behind his back. He'll be as sober as a judge tonight."

The merriment continued apace, but Bebi spotted an anxious vizier's assistant beckoning him over to the door of the State Room.

Mentuhotep watched aslant as the two clerics whispered in earnest discourse. Bebi came rushing back over to the table.

"My Lord, Prince of Kush is marching on the winged chariot, along with the whole of the Kush division. He's found out General Achillas and Princess Iset are on the ship."

"How can this be, Bebi!?"

"Apparently, a Kush slave in the royal kitchens heard a rumour from the staff supplying food and drink to the ship. The slave's gone missing, sire."

Mentuhotep pushed himself awkwardly off his cushion and banged his was-sceptre furiously on the marble floor.

"So my deception to avoid war with Kush has failed. Bring me my war-chariot and my Theban divisions! We march from the East Portal to the winged chariot. We'll defend Achillas and Iset."

The military men all stood to attention.

"Mesehti's company will stand with you, Pharaoh."

"Greatest of Fifty Kashta and the Nubian 3rd cohort will defend the hero Achillas to a man, My Lord."

"And Prince of Kush will feel the sting of my lash, if you need me, Pharaoh."

*

The officers on the bridge of the Vor-maga I watched on the large monitor, observing the scene unfolding below them in the eastern desert outside Thebes. The Kush division had been billeted to the south of the city, in preparation for their victory march back to their homeland south of Mizraim. Now they were moving back north, directly towards the alien sky chariot. The Theban army was massing outside the East Portal and was ready to march the three kilometres east to the ship to intercept the Kush army.

The Chief Engineer shook his head with sadness.

"These sub-Bor-aks don't need much of a reason to fight each other, sir."

The Commander was more circumspect.

"The Bor-ak were once warmongers in many eons past. But we learned to suppress our violent tendencies over time."

"Should I order the AIs to take off and return Achillas and Iset to the safety of the mothership?"

"No, Chief. We need the two spaceships down there, in order to bring up all the sub-Bor-aks we've agreed to take on the Norte Chico expedition. The Prince of Kush has no weapons that can even scratch our ship. What to do is send down the second transport ship and we'll aim to extract the expeditionary party as quickly as possible."

Chapter 39

The Kush division arrived at the sky chariot first and the Prince of Kush ordered an immediate frontal attack, scattering Suti's guards surrounding the ship. Kush archers fired volleys of arrows, blackening the air, but they rebounded ineffectually from the hard, shining metal of the ship. Companies with battering rams smashed at the side of the ship, but to no avail. The Prince exhorted his men to destroy the ship, but even flaming arrows and large fires lit under the ship proved useless. Kush, sitting astride his horse, lost his temper.

"Achillas, you murderer! Come out and face me like a man, you traitorous cur."

On board the ship, Achillas watched what was unfolding outside. He pleaded with the AI robot to let him exit the ship and face his nemesis. Iset clung on to him and cried pitifully.

"No, Achi, please, you can't face the whole Kush army on your own."

The Commander relayed his thoughts from the mothership through the lead AI robot.

"Achillas, Iset's right. Mentuhotep and the Theban army will be here any minute to defend you. I plan to have all of you out of there as quickly as possible. Just hang fire."

A few minutes later, Mentuhotep came charging up on his war-chariot, sand billowing up behind his thundering wheels. Alongside him was a Theban cavalry cohort and to their rear, the infantry of the Thebans and Nubians were coming forward at full trot. General Suti and his guards' cohort, along with Pawura's division massed on the northern flank of the ship. Although, the Prince of Kush was massively outnumbered, he ordered his army to surround the ship and then he rode out to face Pharaoh.

Mentuhotep pulled up his chariot.

"Kush! I do not want war, but if you don't send your division home, you leave me no choice."

"You lied to me, Pharaoh. You told me the murderers were sloping off to Athena, when they're actually hiding here in the ship of Horus."

"I'm not prepared to see my beloved Iset die. She has assured me your son Nekhebet was killed in self-defence."

"If that's the case, sire, then let them be tried fairly in the court of Thebes before you, me, Bebi and a judge."

Mentuhotep shook his head.

"I can't do that, Kush. I've made a pact with the giants of Horus. They've agreed to take Achillas and Iset to a new world far beyond our imaginations. Even you'll never find them."

The Prince's face was like thunder.

"You leave me no choice, My Lord. For the honour of my son, I challenge Pharaoh to a duel. Let's you and me settle this right here."

Bebi rode forward on his horse next to the chariot.

"For god's sake, Mentu. You can't do this. The infantry will be here in five minutes and Suti and Pawura sit on the flank. We'll easily crush the Kush division."

"Hold them back, Bebi. This is about Kush honouring his dead son and me fighting for the right to save my daughter. If a duel saves an all-out war, then so be it. Maybe, I've learned something new about making peace from the Bor-ak."

Mentuhotep turned back to the Prince.

"If a duel settles it, Kush, then let's do it. Your choice of challenge...how d'you choose?"

Prince of Kush bowed reverently to his Pharaoh.

"My Lord, I salute your bravery. I choose horseback, shields and short swords."

"Agreed, Kush."

By the time Mentuhotep and Kush were sitting astride their horses and facing each other about fifty metres apart, the Thebans and Nubians arrived on the battlefield, ready for a fight and chanting for Horus. Bebi held them in check and the two armies sullenly faced each other across the open duelling ground.

Bebi was appointed as intermediary for the duel in the sun and called out to the two senior royals.

"Ready, Pharaoh? Ready, Kush?"

They both nodded and Bebi raised his was-sceptre for all to see. He then dropped it quickly down to his side as the sign to begin. Great cheers rose on both sides as the two horsemen charged at each other. As the sweating horses passed each other the two men smashed their swords at each other with a sparking clang of metal. Arriving at the opposite ends of the duelling ground, they turned their horses and charged once again down the desert field.

As they reached each other a second time, their horses snorting heavily in the heat of the desert, Kush deftly managed to parry Mentuhotep's sword with his shield, whilst he slashed under Mentuhotep's shield, causing a bloody gash on Pharaoh's right arm. There was a momentary hush within the baying armies as they spotted the spray of blood.

The two duellists were on their third charge, when all of a sudden, a sandstorm started billowing up around everyone and everything. The two horses charged into the billowing clouds of dust and disappeared from everyone's view. Mesehti looked heavenward and shouted.

"Look! Another winged chariot."

The second spaceship was coming down to land close to the first and the terrified soldiers of Kush scattered in all four directions. Bebi moved the Theban and Nubian forces back to allow the ship to land. It landed quietly and effortlessly, but with sand blowing everywhere. Soldiers turned away from the sandstorm or covered their eyes and mouths with pieces of cloth or rags.

Minutes later, as the dust settled, all eyes squinted back to the duelling ground. The two panting horses stood rider-less. They were both startled by the giant ship and had thrown their mounts. Mentuhotep lay motionless on his back and Prince of Kush lay on top with Pharaoh's sword having skewered right through him as he fell. Mentuhotep had been knocked out and lay unconscious. Kush was stone dead, blood seeping out of his lifeless body. Seeing his Prince had been killed, the Lieutenant Commander of the Kush division ordered his troops back into line.

"The duel's all over, men. Let's go home to our families in Kush."

As the Kush division fell into line and slowly started marching south, the Thebans and Nubians rhythmically banged their swords and spears on their shields as a token of respect. The Kush had fought alongside them at the battle of the Nile and all were relieved another terrible battle had been averted. As they marched south, the Kush division began singing the Theban hymn as a mark of respect to their comrades-in-arms.

Mentuhotep regained consciousness and pulled himself up to great cheering. He looked down on the man who was once his friend and ally and he wept a tear. Bebi ordered the cavalry, the Thebans and Nubians to return to their billets.

"Bebi, Kush fell on me by accident. We'll arrange for him to have a military funeral and be buried with honour at the royal necropolis at Abydos."

The door of the first ship whooshed open and Iset and Achillas came running down the metallic ramp. Iset threw herself into Mentuhotep's arms and he winced as she brushed against his seeping wound.

"Father, father! It's over. We can all return to Thebes."

Mentuhotep held Iset at arm's length and looked at her sadly.

"It's not as simple as that, Iset. There would still have to be a trial and the likelihood is you and Achillas would be found guilty. Pharaoh must uphold the laws of Mizraim or no longer be a god-king in the eyes of his people."

"But, father, you're Pharaoh. You can order a court to find us innocent."

Achillas spoke softly.

"Issi, we cannot tie Pharaoh's hands behind his back, or else he'll lose face across all of Mizraim. We must depart with the giants of Horus to the new world of the Norte Chico and start our new life together as husband and wife."

Chapter 40

Achillas and Iset were married by the two eunuch priests on board the gaily decorated bridge of the Vor-maga I. In attendance were Iset's mother, Princess Meketaten, Ruth, Meseh-ti, Kashta, the Nubian tracker and the two viziers. The Mizris and Nubians were completely in awe of their surroundings and Iset felt this was even more palatial a wedding venue than marrying her betrothed Achillas in the Theban Royal Palace. The Bor-ak Commander, his Chief Engineer, Ship's Doctor and the female Navigator also acted as slightly bemused witnesses.

Mentuhotep had sent aboard a great Mizri wedding banquet, which was supplemented by the less appetising pre-packed pouches of food for the Bor-ak guests. The Commander was mightily impressed with this sub-Bor-ak ceremony.

"We Bor-ak had nothing like this in our old culture back on the red traveller. Males and females just took their mates without any ceremony. But, I like it…and today, I think we have learned something new from the blue travellers."

He turned to the Navigator, having admired her from afar for a very long time.

"Navigator, will you be my wife?"

"I will, Commander."

A great cheer arose from the guests.

*

The following sunrise, the two AI-manned spaceships took the Mizri expedition down to the new world of the Norte Chico people on the coast of the great eastern sea. Achillas and Iset and the rest of the expedition were welcomed by the Norte Chicans as gods from the heavens as they alighted from the two winged chariots of Horus. Their arrival in the chariots of the gods would become part of the mythology of the Norte Chico people and handed down to the civilisations that followed them, such as the Incas, Mayans and Aztecs.

*

The following sunrise, with the moon on the far side of the planet, the Commander looked wistfully down on the blue traveller for the last time, a tear forming on his eyelid. He would miss these sub-Bor-aks. They had an astonishing future ahead of them, with many difficult lessons to be learned, but they were survivors.

"Okay, wife…I mean, Navigator. Fusion drive level one. Take us out of orbit and aim for the slingshot around Vor. Let's venture out into deep space and find our own New World."

Epilogue

Mentuhotep II (Ancient Egyptian: Mn-ṯw-ḥtp, meaning 'Mentu is satisfied'), also known under his prenomen Nephepetre (Ancient Egyptian: Nb-ḥpt-Rˁ, meaning 'The Lord of the rudder is Ra'), was an ancient Egyptian pharaoh circa 2061–2010 BCE, the sixth ruler of the Eleventh Dynasty. He is credited with reuniting Egypt, thus ending the turbulent First Intermediate Period and becoming the first pharaoh of the Middle Kingdom. He reigned for 51 years, according to the Turin King List. Mentuhotep II had succeeded his father Intef III on the throne and he was in turn succeeded by his own son Mentuhotep III.

Mentuhotep II ascended Egypt's throne in the Upper Egyptian city of Thebes during the First Intermediate Period. Egypt was not finally unified during this time, and the Tenth Dynasty, the rival to Mentuhotep's Eleventh, ruled Lower Egypt from the capital Herakleopolis. Following the Herakleopolitan King's desecration of the sacred and ancient royal necropolis of Abydos in Upper Egypt in the fourteenth year of Mentuhotep's reign, the Pharaoh sent his armies north to conquer Lower Egypt. Continuing from his late father Intef III's conquests, Mentuhotep succeeded in unifying his country, probably shortly before his 39th year on the throne. In recognition of the unification, in regnal year 39, he changed his titulary to Shematawy (Ancient Egyptian: Šmˁ-t3-wj, meaning 'He who unifies the two lands').

Following the unification, Mentuhotep II reformed Egypt's government. In order to reverse the decentralization of power, which contributed to the collapse of the Old Kingdom and marked the First Intermediate Period, he centralized the state in Thebes to strip his nomarchs of some of their powers over the regions. Mentuhotep II also created new governmental posts whose occupants were Theban men loyal to him, giving Pharaoh more control over his country. Officials from the capital travelled the country regularly to control regional leaders.

Mentuhotep II was buried at the Theban necropolis of Deir el-Bahri. His mortuary temple was one of Mentuhotep II's most ambitious building projects, and which included several architectural and religious innovations. It included terraces and covered walkways around the central structure, and it was the first mortuary temple that identified Pharaoh with the god Osiris. His temple inspired several later mortuary temples, such as those of Hatshepsut and Thutmose III of the Eighteenth Dynasty.

Reference: *Wikipedia*.

About the author

Derek Beaugarde is a pseudonym for his science-fiction publications and Derek Niven is used by the author John McGee, a member of ASGRA, for his factual and genealogical footballing history publications. John McGee, aka *The Two Dereks*, was born in 1956 in the railway village of Corkerhill, Glasgow. He attended Mosspark Primary and Allan Glen's schools. In the 1930s, the late, great actor Sir Dirk Bogarde spent two unhappy years at Allan Glen's School when he was a pupil named Derek Niven van den Bogaerde. The observant reader will readily discern the origin of the two pseudonyms. After spending 34 years in the rail industry in train planning and accountancy, John McGee retired in 2007.

In 2012, the idea for his apocalyptic sci-fi novel first emerged, and 2084 The End of Days © Derek Beaugarde was published by Corkerhill Press in 2016. This was followed by Pride of the Lions © Derek Niven published in 2017, Pride of the Jocks © Derek Niven, foreword by Kathleen Murdoch, published in 2018, Pride of the Bears © Derek Niven published in 2020 and Pride of the Hearts © Derek Niven published in 2021. The space opera novellas 2112 Revelation © Derek Beaugarde and 2048 BCE The Eye of Horus © Derek Beaugarde were simultaneously published in eBook format on 1 May 2023, with paperback versions in 2024 and 2025 respectively.

Published books by Derek Beaugarde

Published books by Derek Niven

PRIDE OF
THE BEARS
The untold story of the men and women
who made the Barça Bears
DEREK NIVEN

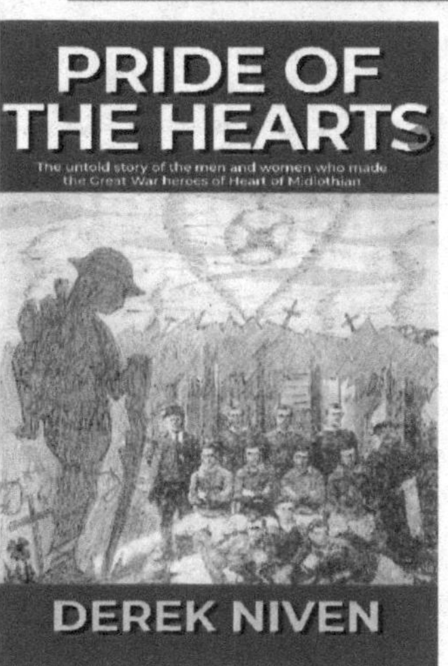

PRIDE OF
THE HEARTS
The untold story of the men and women who made
the Great War heroes of Heart of Midlothian
DEREK NIVEN

9 781739 392956